The Eya....

Journal

Linda Copp

L.R. Price Publications Ltd

Published in Great Britain by

L.R. Price Publications Ltd, 2021

27 Old Gloucester Street,

London, WC1N 3AX

www.lrpricepublications.com

Cover artwork by Janelle Hope

L.R. Price Publications Ltd Copyright © 2022

Story by Linda Copp

Linda Coppy Copyright © 2022

ISBN-13: 9781739805265

Dedication

This book is dedicated to the two hundred and sixty residents of Eyam, who between September 1665 and November 1666, fell victim to the plague.

The Eyam

Journal

Linda Copp

The Eyam Journal

Remember man

As thou goest by,

As thou art now,

Even once was I;

As I doe now

So must thou lie,

Remember man,

That thou must die.

Epitaph at Riley graves, Eyam.

To my dear friend Emmott,

I offer you this parchment and
   quill so that you might practise
   that which we have studied
   together.
Joyful Yuletide greetings and my
   very best wishes always,

Catherine Mompesson.
Christmas 1664.

4th June 1665

It has been almost a year now since Catherine and Mr. Mompesson alighted from that fine carriage and first put foot down in Eyam. How glad I am that the good Lord chose to bring them here. Catherine is as delicate as a flower yet has one of the biggest and strongest hearts I have known. There was, of course, much talk amongst us and much activity in the rectory prior to their arrival. It was rumoured that Mr. William Mompesson and his wife were a young, married couple with two small children, a boy and a girl, coming from Scalby near Scarborough. That day, as they drove through the village, all stopped to try and catch a glimpse of the new rector and his family.

The carriage drew up opposite the rectory gates; Mr. Mompesson gallantly offered his hand to steady his wife's descent. The housemaid, Bridget, carried little Elizabeth, still heavy from sleep, in her arms. George in his excitement jumped down unnoticed and tottered straight across the road, right into the path of Mr. Howe's horse and cart. Being of an ill-tempered nature, Mr. Howe, unimpressed by status as is his wont, took to shouting and blaspheming, quite startling the young child so that he became quite frozen to the spot. I, being on my journey home from the market house, from whence I had procured some eggs, witnessed the whole scene. Clumsily, the eggs were dropped as I swept the poor child, who had now started to fret and cry, up into my arms and delivered him safely back to his parents.

It was thus that I first made acquaintance with William and Catherine Mompesson. He was a tall, slim man with a fine and noble nose, light of hair and red of cheek. She was of tender beauty, a slight, frail creature that looked as a mere breeze might unbalance her. Her complexion was pale as milk and her blonde hair was tucked neatly under her cap. As she looked at me straight on with those kindly, searching blue eyes of hers, I judged her to be not much older than myself. Feeling suddenly rather self-conscious of my somewhat ruffled appearance, I hastened to smooth out my skirts and to tame my unruly hair behind my ears. Remarking that she had unnerved me somewhat, her mouth broke into a wide smile. She then insisted that I should accompany her into the rectory to replenish my stock of eggs, which she assured me she had provision of in the kitchen larder.

Catherine flitted about, and first finding some milk, she put it in a pan to warm. She then searched again for the eggs, chatting all the while about her former home in Scalby. After a few minutes she exited the larder with eggs in hand and persuaded me to stay and partake of the milk with her; she being thirsty after her long journey. So it was that we spent the first of what was to be many an hour at that kitchen table, nestling a hot drink in our hands. So forthright and honest a soul I have yet to meet. So unguarded was she in her discourse, that one might mistake her directness for naivety, or even simpleness of mind, which indeed could not be further from the truth. Catherine, as I know her now, is indeed rather complex in character and her mind an equal to any man I know.

I left that day not only armed with a fresh supply of eggs, but with the newly acquired position of 'house help', as Catherine called it. Even though their own housemaid had accompanied them from their former dwelling, I was to be employed in assisting her in the looking after of the children and in the undertaking of some of the domestic tasks. The extra wage I have brought to the family has indeed been significant, us being nine in total, but more valuable than that has been her instruction and friendship. Fate happened me to stumble not only upon a position that day, but also upon a patient tutor and trusted confidant. An auspicious day indeed, that I have oft since given thanks for in prayer.

8th June 1665

This morning I helped Catherine with the laundry. Once it was scrubbed, rung and pressed we hung it upon the line in the garden to dry, it being perfect drying weather; warm and breezy. Catherine and I then tended the garden whilst George and Elizabeth amused themselves with pots and pans filled with water that had been brought out from the house. Catherine has instructed me well and I can now recognise most flowers by name and correctly determine them from common weeds. So it was, we spent a pleasant morning pottering in the borders whilst chatting and listening to the children's happy play.

Mid-day Catherine fetched an old blanket which she spread under the shade of the old ash tree, and there we shared bread and cheese with the children. After, we sat a while and admired the diversity of colour and form that was offered us by the many plants so tenderly cared for. What joy Catherine takes from her garden. She might sit there all day picking out each individual flower, shrub and bush and making mental note of any change or growth it has undergone. Each plant is so lovingly dealt with and so carefully nurtured, for as she once told me, she sees them all to be small creations of God.

This afternoon, once I had taken leave of my duties, it being such a fine day, Rowland and I took a stroll up through the woods and onto the ridge that overlooks the valley towards Stoney Middleton. We took shade under the old sycamore tree. Sat there, leant against a twisted, fallen branch, we allowed the sun's warmth to penetrate our skin. The sunlight made such patterns as it played upon our closed eyelids through the breeze-blown leaves. Their faint rustling and the birdsong were the only sounds to be heard, interrupted on occasion by the distant bleat of sheep. We lay like this a while.

I was nigh lost in reverie when I felt his arm pull upon my waist. The light and the warmth were then eclipsed as I felt his lips upon mine. He felt so close, he, wrapped up in me; wrapped up in one another. It was warm and safe and I felt within me the stirrings of love, a kind of soft buzzing, in the very pit of my stomach. We were at peace; we felt contentment. Laying there, thus, we were transported for a while, to somewhere without time or distraction. Heavy, as in sleep, our limbs warmed and relaxed. We smelt the lightly cloying air and the soil. We breathed it into us. Thus we remained, suspended.

At once, from somewhere not so far away, a bird batted its wings upon the compacted earth. Our eyes opened and we were both at once affronted by the brightness of the raw daylight. The spell was reluctantly broken. We held gaze for a while and then I rested my head upon his chest.

He squeezed my hand in his, and mine squeezed back. Our bodies, it seemed, had a secret language of their own. We lay there still, dreamily. Time slowed to a mere trickle as we let the sun and the warm stirrings of the air tentatively brush their gentle caresses upon our faces.

12th June 1665.

The summer, thus far being so verily temperate, has afforded us many an afternoon on the hillsides or in the delf near the brooks and rivulets. Catherine's two, George and little Elizabeth, have taken quite a shining to my brother Richard and the girls. They spend hours paddling in the water, playing in the grass or rolling down the hillocks. Ellen and Elizabeth, being the eldest of my siblings, keep a watchful eye on the little ones whilst Catherine and I steal an hour or so to read together.

I have confided in Catherine that I have made a journal of her yuletide gift to me. Upon this disclosure she insisted that I should borrow her copy of Thomas Blount's 'Glossographia'. I have since spent many an hour perusing its pages. Some words are completely new to me. Some are very technical in term. There are those limited to certain districts or even derived from other countries entirely. A complex definition is given for each word and ultimately its origins are expounded. How amazing to me it is, that words are all linked and derived from other words. Furthermore, there is much common ground to be found in many languages foreign to that of our own. So it is, we are all linked and joined together by our common linguistic heritage. I have been completely spellbound by my new discovery; it opening up a whole new world to me. I have taken to carrying it around with me, whenever and wherever possible, so that if the opportunity arises, I might steal a few precious minutes in its company.

Catherine and I still manage to find time between and after duties to continue my studies. Oft times, during the long, grey winter months we sit by candlelight, in front of the hearth, at the rectory's kitchen table. Catherine flatters me in pronouncing that I am a quick learner and that my reading and writing might now be equal to her own. Little does she suspect that at home, once my tasks are completed and I have settled the little ones to their beds, I fill every given spare minute with practise. Such is my desire and joy to be literate. This journal and quill enjoys little rest when my hands are otherwise unengaged.

Catherine and I took the children to the brook-side today. Mr Mompesson had fashioned them some nets of a sort from muslin pieces secured to the end of willow sticks. They amused themselves the whole afternoon in catching various insects and small fish, placing them in the otherwise idle coal pails. How the little ones squealed to find something trapped in their nets.

Indeed their excitement was at times so great that the poor captured creature was oft able to make its escape, such was their distraction. Their disappointment on remarking the evasion was short-lived indeed, as there seemed to be a plethora of water life ready to take the newly-liberated creature's place. Alice, of course, being so very cautious by nature, was very hesitant to step into the running brook. She could not be persuaded to take off her shoes, so fished from the side instead with seemingly equal success.

At lunch time we sat down to a feast of cold meats, bread and cheese. The children, once their hunger had been sated, immediately became impatient and restless. In haste, with food still in their mouths, they ran to resume their activities. It was then that Catherine enquired after Rowland. I replied that he was very well and duly thanked her for her concern. The averting of my gaze and the warm redness which I felt creep into my neck and cheeks, no doubt gave rise to the knowing smile she gave me. I told her then that I was indeed very fond of him and him of me, and that we had talked of a possible future together now he was secure to take over the running of his father's flour mill. This verily tickled Catherine who became quite excitable.

"Oh Emmott," she declared, "what a pretty bride you will make... William will be thrilled to marry you... Just imagine..."

At which I grew even more flustered and swore her to secrecy insisting that, as yet, we were not even betrothed. Fortunately, at that point, I was rescued by Sarah who informed us that George had fallen into the brook and was quite drenched through. This event obviously sent poor Alice into a fit of hysteria, whilst it amused Richard quite to the point that tears of laughter rolled down his cheeks. It was Ellen who had helped George in emerging from the water. She was now sat with him upon the bank, her arm in consolation around his shoulder. Catherine thanked Ellen and then gathered George into her arms. Sarah and Elizabeth arranged the remaining foods and utensils into the pannier. I picked up the picnic blanket and passed it to Catherine, who proceeded to wrap George in it, more for comfort than for warmth. Ellen took little Elizabeth's hand and Sarah occupied herself in calming Alice. I carried the pannier and nets. Thus organised, we made our journey home.

18th June 1665

It being the Sabbath, Ellen, Elizabeth and I helped Mother to bathe and ready the little ones for church. Richard kicked up a fuss, as usual, at having his face scrubbed and his hair combed through. Alice dawdled, lost in her own world, so that she needed much encouragement to be prepared afore the church bells set to summon us. Father, as always, had cleaned the shoes and had laid them at the threshold in order of size, as is his habit. Once we were all scrubbed, clothed and shod, his short, broad figure led us purposefully across the road to church. Mother brought up the rear with baby Joseph in arms, ensuring all were rounded up and heading in the right direction.

The service was as engaging as always; Mr. Mompesson is a lively speaker. He is able to capture effortlessly the attention of his congregation. Thus being so unlike his predecessor, Mr. Adams, who was by contrast rather drab and seemed to hold as little interest himself in his words as did the rest of those gathered before him. None could fail to notice the impact that Mr. Mompesson, and indeed Catherine, have had upon the church and its congregation this past year or about, both being greatly respected by young and old alike. All have witnessed the rise in attendance and remarked upon the rector's dynamic style of preaching and the sincerity of his words. Those who, at the onset, doubted the aptness of his appointment, giving his lack of years and experience as cause, have indeed long since been silenced. He has indeed directness in his message, preaching of a God who is all loving and forgiving, rather than one who judges and wreaks vengeance. On terminating his sermon one feels uplifted and joyous. All fear is discarded. There is left an inspiration to act upon his words: 'Seeking the God within us all,' as he states it. There can be no doubt that we are the happier, the richer and much the wiser, in receiving and acting upon the lessons he blesses us with.

After the service, as is our habit, all stopped a while outside to exchange pleasantries and items of news. Our Elizabeth, Elizabeth Blackwell and the Talbot girls, Bridget and Mary, huddled under one of the many linden trees as is their custom. In their small huddle they conversed excitedly, breaking out into occasional laughter. I minded Alice and Richard as Mother and our neighbour, Mrs. Thorpe, mithered over the state of collapse of the stone wall that separates our two properties. This dispute has been ongoing for many a week now and as yet, no satisfactory decision as to whose responsibility it is to repair it has been reached. It is, however, mostly done with humour, as being lifelong friends there can be no real animosity between the two.

As we started to leave, I was rather surprised to remark Father deep in conversation with Marshall Howe; he who seldom has a word for anyone. Mr. Howe, being so tall and my father by contrast being rather short in stature meant that Father had his neck craned somewhat, in order to retain eye contact. Both were looking rather stern. In between the distractions of the children hanging from my legs, I unsuccessfully strained to eavesdrop in a bid to ascertain what might be amiss.

My curiosity was soon abated on reaching the house. Up until he had closed the door, Father had managed to retain his composure, though from the redness of his face, the gritted teeth, clenched fists and hurried, definite pace, we all knew he was battling hard to do so. We huddled like scared rabbits in the kitchen, waiting to find out which one of us had offended him so. At length, Richard was told to stay and the rest of us ordered to leave the room. Mother accompanied us into the small, dark parlour as we listened to Father let loose his anger. It seems that Richard had been spotted by Mr. Howe, in his garden, crawling along the branch of one of his fruit trees. He accused Richard of attempting to steal some cherries, though none had seen to be taken. Mr. Howe had complained to Father how the ripening fruit would now be bruised and damaged and although he could not prove that theft had occurred, threatened to report Richard for trespassing. Richard remained silent as Father repeated the assertions of Mr. Howe. He remained silent too during the beating that ensued, though we heard clearly the crack of

Father's belt as it made cruel contact with the top of his thighs.

Richard limped out of the kitchen, red faced and with a silent tear rolling down his cheek. He sniffed on seeing us and then, like an injured animal, went to find a quiet corner in which to lick his wounds. Shortly, Mother followed after him, carrying a small cloth bathed in salt water. I winced to think of the smarting and the stinging now to be endured. I cannot believe that Richard chose Mr. Howe's garden to violate. It shows either incredible bravery or pure stupidity. An adventurous spirit must be channelled along the correct path from the onset, says Father, else it will lead us to calamity. There is truth, of course, in his words but I do wish, for his own and all our sakes, that Richard would have been blessed with at least a smattering of Alice's more reflective and over-cautious nature.

25th June 1665

This morning at the rectory I assisted Catherine in the changing of all the bedclothes. After, I was occupied in the scrubbing of the hall floor and stairs. Bridget, the housemaid, polished the wooden banisters and washed down all of the doors, whilst Catherine played upon her clavichord. Some of the tunes I had never heard before. Mr. Mompesson having recently returned from a visit to Manchester had, to Catherine's delight, acquired her several new scores of music. The melodies, though at times stilted as Catherine faltered in her playing, certainly rendered the chores less monotonous.

On leaving the rectory I wandered down to The Cross, to procure some supplies for Mother's larder from the market house. As I passed The Miners Croft I perceived a soft sobbing from behind the stone wall. Wondering, as I did, what might be amiss and who might be so heavy of heart to lament so, I placed a foot upon an outcrop of rock and hauled myself up so that I might peer over the top. Sat with their backs to me, upon this piece of common land, were young Edythe Carter and Ann Bagshaw. It was Edythe who was in tears and Ann, who with one arm around her shoulders, endeavoured to console her. Seeing them thus, and so earnest in discourse, I did not want to disturb them and so, with caution, I lowered myself once again onto the road below.

Ann and Edythe had been inseparable since childhood, yet a more unlikely coupling you could not expect to encounter. Edythe is exuberant and carefree by nature and possesses something of a wild and rebellious streak within her. Ann, by contrast, is quiet, cautious and so guarded in her speech and actions, that few know much of her thoughts; or indeed of herself. I do believe that Edythe alone knows her real nature, for even her sole surviving parent takes little interest in her. Ann resides at Bagshaw Hall with her mother, Mrs. Bagshaw, whom everyone knows by surname alone. Edythe comes from much humbler an abode and is one of eight children, though it seems she is better loved and more cared for than Ann. Physically too, they are as chalk and cheese. Ann being a tall, extremely thin and particularly plain young lady, whilst Edythe is the prettiest of things, with her dark, wild, curling hair and brightly shining, brown eyes, that betray equally her love of life and her intelligence.

As I continued my journey to the market house, I could not help but wonder what the cause of such distress might be. The anxiety and gravity that lay in Ann's regard suggested that whatever it might be, it was not of little consequence.

This afternoon, I accompanied Mother and Ellen to the oven where we baked two loaves and an egg pie. Ellen amused both Mother and me with the recounting of the story of Mary and

Bridget's father, Mr. Talbot, whom they had witnessed yesterday in hot pursuit of one of the hogs that had escaped from its enclosure. Apparently the hog did not take kindly to being chased and cornered, and on more than one occasion it took to charging at poor Mr. Talbot, with a look upon its face that Ellen described as 'an intent to do him harm'. The aggressive beast was only tamed and reinstated in its pen when Mrs. Talbot, all of a fluster, called upon the men of the neighbouring farmstead to join the chase armed with wooden stakes and sticks!

1st July 1665

It being such a fine summer morning, after service we all remained a little longer before the church than is our custom. Mother and Father were engaged in conversation with Mr. and Mrs. Thorpe, whose cottage adjoins our own. Father was commenting on the splendid abundance of vegetables they had both this year managed to cultivate, in their sizeable plots situated in the rear gardens. The younger children fidgeted impatiently at their sides.

Catherine and I stood sheltered in the shade of the church entrance. Opposite, Mr. Mompesson exchanged pleasantries with the last of his emerging congregation. Mrs. Bagshaw was, as is oft times the case, last to exit, so ensuring her the undivided attention of the rector. Hovering behind her right shoulder, her daughter Ann like some pale shadow, followed.

I have always considered Mrs. Bagshaw to present a rather frightening figure. Indeed, as a child I found myself to shy away from her and would peek at her, surreptitiously, from the safety of Mother's skirts, so overbearing is she in both build and demeanour. She is tall for a woman, yet still her ample bosom and generous rear seem quite disproportionate to her stature, these being only exaggerated by the particularly upright stance she adopts. Her features remain always in the same harsh expression, exhibiting a slight look of displeasure, as if she had just partaken of some milk that has turned. Somehow her voice carries itself above all others, though she speaks not in raised tones, but rather with a vocal projection as used by the players who visit to act out stories at Wakes' tide. I can only assume that her daughter, Ann, must be more akin to her father who passed when she was but an infant, for she is a frail, pallid creature, whose voice is seldom heard at all.

Thus it was that we had not to strain to overhear Mrs. Bagshaw's exchange with the good reverend. After a rather sycophantic appraisal as to the merits of the morning service and its delivery, Mrs. Bagshaw, who was quite undeterred and seemingly oblivious to the reverend's growing unease and embarrassment, (betrayed as it was by his somewhat faltering composure), barely hesitated to draw breath before revealing her intent.

It emerged that her agenda on this occasion was to secure a post as governess for her daughter Ann, who, in her humble opinion, being blessed as she was with such a kindly disposition and adept in intellect, would indeed be ideal for just such a role. So it was that she enquired as to whether the good reverend would be in need himself of such a service, or indeed if he might know of any relative, friend or acquaintance of equally good standing, let it be understood, who might be interested in securing just such an asset so as to complement their household.

I perceived poor Catherine to tense at the conjecture, obviously quite unsure of what the retort of her husband might be to this rather unnerving solicitation. Fortunately, the length of Mrs. Bagshaw's address had procured the good reverend more than enough time to recover his composure. To Catherine's discernible relief he politely explained that, at present, they had no need of a governess, his wife being not only entirely competent but also more than willing to undertake the instruction of their children herself. As to his knowing of any persons who might be looking to fill such a position, unfortunately none came immediately to mind. However, he would most definitely take heed of her kind offer, and were he made aware of any suitable placements arising, he would most certainly notify her forthwith. Upon which Mrs. Bagshaw offered abrupt thanks and, seeming somewhat deflated, bid good day. She thence made a rather hasty departure with her daughter, whose normally wan complexion now appeared slightly flushed, in tow.

Catherine and her husband thereupon exchanged a look of bemused relief. I could not help but to convey my amusement at the recent turn of events, for try as I might I was unable to suppress the wry smile I could feel taking form and then proceeding to install itself upon my face. On remarking my expression, Catherine followed suit and it was as much as we could do to stifle our giggles. Although attempting to generate a look of disapproval, even the rector allowed himself a fleeting display of solidarity, breaking momentarily, as he did, into a broad grin.

10th July 1665

Whilst my sister Elizabeth and I were at our piece work this evening, she told me that it is said that Edythe Carter and Edward Taylor are to be married. She is only just of legal age and it is rumoured that the hastiness of their actions is due to the fact that she is with child. As soon as I heard these words, a picture came into my mind of poor Edythe sobbing behind the croft wall, and of Ann Bagshaw's attempts to console her. Elizabeth then proceeded to tell me that Mr. Carter, Edythe's father, was intent upon her visiting the Wise Woman in Bakewell to have the infant forced from her belly. Upon the hearing of which, Mrs. Carter pleaded with him to show some mercy. We have all heard told of many an unfortunate girl, whom in making such a journey has thereafter fallen ill through infection or loss of blood and eventually perished in agony. Thankfully he was eventually persuaded to relinquish his notion, aided no doubt by the timely proposal of marriage from Edward.

It is well-known that Edward and Edythe have a great fondness for each other. He has followed her around adoringly since childhood and she has always a smile for him and has never turned him away or spoken unkindly to him. Edward's affections were always obviously stronger than those of Edythe. One could never really imagine her being tied in anyway, to anyone or anything, being as she is rather like a butterfly upon the wind that flits here and there, landing momentarily only to take flight again almost immediately.

Poor Edythe, if it be true what worry and dread she must have felt these last weeks or months even. I remember stories told of Bessie

Higgens, who at seventeen was made an outcast after giving birth to a baby girl out of wedlock. It is said that the two of them were driven from the village and not knowing where to settle, she somehow managed to reach Manchester with her babe in arms, thinking she might be able to hide her past in the anonymity of a big city. It is uncertain as to what happened after, though some say they ended up in the poor house, the infant and mother separated, and that both perished shortly thereafter. It is often heard said that there are few who reach old age in the poor house and fewer still who ever leave, unless it be carried out in a box. No one ever knew who the father of the poor child might be. Bessie remained loyal, refused to say and took her secret to the grave no doubt. I hope his conscience on hearing of her demise haunted him and if he is alive, does so still, for he lifted not a finger to aid her.

12th July 1665

At the rectory this morning we opened the double doors from the kitchen to the garden. Catherine and I baked some pies and began a potage afresh as we watched Elizabeth and George amuse themselves in the sunshine. I asked her if she had heard of the intended union of Edward and Edythe. She told me that indeed she had, for the parents and married couple-to-be were at the rectory just last week, enquiring as to whether Mr. Mompesson would oversee the small ceremony. She tells how Mr. and Mrs. Carter, alongside Edward and Edythe, had all stood rather nervously in the lounge. Mr. Carter first broached the subject explaining that the young couple wished to be married as soon as the licence had been obtained. It was as Catherine carried in the refreshments on a small tray, that Mr. Mompesson asked if he might enquire as to the reason of them all being in such haste to undertake such a ceremony. Catherine said that with a firm frankness of voice and head held high, Edythe thereupon answered,

'Yes Reverend you may. I believe I am carrying his child. We know we have sinned and we have begged that God might forgive us each day. We love each other dearly and have always meant to be together, we have both decided to take the necessary steps to do what is best for our unborn child'.

Mr. Mompesson at first seemed quite taken aback by the forthrightness of the confession. He was rather expecting to hear that the weather were to be a determining factor or that important relatives, only being able to secure leave from their labours during that time, to be the reason offered. Catherine said that she herself almost dropped the tray; such was her shock at the revelation and at the honesty and directness of the statement. Yet Edythe stood fast holding Edward's hand in hers, her large, brown eyes as innocent as a child's. Catherine admitted that she could not help but feel some admiration towards this young woman for her courage and the strength of her conviction.

"Let us say it is 'possible' you may be with child but let us keep that 'possibility' between us and within these four walls. We may undertake your troth-plight here this very day. I will post the Banns upon the church door in the morn. As you know, three weeks thence, I can and will, officially join you as man and wife, as I believe that to be the best outcome for all here involved. You have asked for God's forgiveness you say and the sin you have committed is, I believe, a sin born out of love rather than out of greed or hate. If he forgives you, as he does all who ask him in earnest, then how can I not?"

Upon hearing these words, Catherine recalled how the tension in the room fell away. All gathered seemed mightily relieved and expressed their gratitude if not once, then a hundred times. Mrs. Carter took to sobbing into her kerchief.

Edward and Edythe held each other tight and close for a very long while, whilst Mr. Carter would not relinquish the firm grip that he now had of the reverend's hand. Catherine described the scene as 'truly heart-warming' and told of how her eyes brimmed with tears of pride for her husband who had proved himself, once again, to be of a fair, tolerant and wholly philanthropic nature.

Catherine was asked by Edythe to also be witness to the hand-fasting. Hastily, she pulled a length of crimson ribbon from her sewing basket and with a knife fetched hurriedly from the kitchen, divided it into two equal lengths so they might have a small gift to exchange as is the custom. Thus sorted, Edward and Edythe clasped their right hands together and looking each other face on, the ceremony commenced.

"I. Edward Taylor, take thee, Edythe Carter, to be my wedded wife, 'til death us do part and thereto I plight thee my troth."

"I, Edythe Carter, take thee, Edward Taylor, to be my wedded husband, 'til death us do part and thereto I plight thee my troth."

Upon completion, the ribbons were exchanged and all left the room with a smile upon their face and no doubt a lightness in their hearts.

I was, of course, sworn to secrecy as to the why-fore of such a hasty union being made, and not a word of this shall fall from my lips. The following day, as promised, the Banns was nailed to the church door. The whole village is full of gossip and conjecture but no one can prove her condition. They have committed no heinous crime, nor have they acted upon whim or indeed without depth of feeling as do those men that pay visit to houses of ill-repute. They are to be married and I for one, wish them happiness.

18th July 1665.

Catherine, Bridget and I dusted and polished the rectory from top to bottom today.

Before taking my leave, Catherine and I sat in the rectory garden a while. Catherine told me that Mrs. Bagshaw, accompanied by her daughter Ann, had paid visit to the rectory last evening. Catherine had been sat in the garden reading. Bridget must have opened the door to them and announced their arrival to Mr. Mompesson. They were shown into the sitting room and Catherine, who was installed below the open window, unwittingly overheard the whole exchange which she recounted to me this midday. I will record it here, in as near to her own words as memory permits.

"My dear Reverend, what a fine evening we are blessed with! My daughter Ann and I could not resist the opportunity to take some air, it being so gloriously clement. We have just returned from a most delightful visit to the delf. On approaching the rectory we thought we might be so decadent as to pay our most revered rector an unexpected social call. I do hope that you consider us an amiable intrusion upon your respite, Reverend?"

"Why, Mrs. Bagshaw, Miss Bagshaw, it is indeed an unexpected pleasure. Would you both care for some refreshment after your excursion?"

"That is very kind Reverend but we would not have you go to any trouble on our account and we promise not to take up too much of your precious time. We know how busy you must be in perfecting your sermon. Oh, how we both look forward with anticipation to hearing them and never do we find ourselves disappointed!"

"That is very kind. I was indeed just about to retire to the study to work upon the service for this Sunday."

"May I be so bold as to enquire as to the message of this upcoming service Reverend? I am always keen to know upon what topic we might be so admirably instructed. It would afford me meanwhile, the opportunity to dedicate myself wholeheartedly to the considered reflection it no doubt deserves!"

"The subject matter Mrs. Bagshaw is one very close to my heart and, as is illustrated in the Good Book, to our Lord's also, it being tolerance Mrs. Bagshaw."

"Ah. Tolerance indeed, how very splendid! Well, I will search my soul with diligence my dear Reverend."

"I am pleased that you will pay weight to the subject Mrs. Bagshaw, for I fear at times we are all guilty of finding this quality somewhat lacking in our hearts."

"Yes indeed, indeed... It is told you were paid visit by the Carters and Edward Taylor this evening past Reverend. I do hope nothing is amiss and that they all fare well?"

"Yes, it is true that they called on a family matter."

"A family matter? I do hope the cause was not of a hapless nature, Reverend. As you may be aware, my dear daughter Ann and Edythe Carter are very close and have been since childhood, as unfathomable as that might seem!"

"Yes, I am aware of that Mrs. Bagshaw and as such I am sure that Ann will be one of the first to know."

"Oh indeed Reverend, she has already been confided in as to the liaison betwixt Edythe and Edward and their intention to wed."

"Why then Mrs. Bagshaw do you enquire as to whether the visit were of a 'hapless' nature?"

"Well Reverend, how might I express this? It being a matter of such a delicate nature, especially to a woman of my moral standing and before the ears of such an innocent, as is my dear Ann, but there is talk that the cause that mitigates this rather hasty decision is perpetrated by a vice of the most vile and sinful nature; a bestial act undertaken through a submission to the flesh and a vulgar disregard for all morality. Indeed, I have forbidden my sweet Ann from having any further contact with the wench. To think that she too might have been corrupted! The very thought. Oh, such shame!"

"Mrs. Bagshaw, I have been asked to join the two as man and wife. They have told me that they wish to spend the rest of their lives together and I have agreed to bless the union. Indeed, their hand fasting is already undertaken. I do not condone listening to idle gossip and even less to fuelling it. Now if you would be so kind, I do have that sermon to finish. Thank you for your unexpected visit and I will no doubt see you in church on Sunday. I do hope that you will find the service both instructive and enlightening."

"Oh, no doubt, as always Reverend, as always."

"'I will have Bridget show you out. Thank you Mrs. Bagshaw, Miss Bagshaw. I wish you good night."

"On the contrary Reverend, thank you for your hospitality and may you receive inspiration from above for your work this evening, until Sunday then. Goodnight."

The visitors thus hastily dispatched with, Mr. Mompesson retired to his study with a slam of the door.

The reverend oft repeats that it is not our role to be the judge of others but rather to see each and every one of us as 'God's work in progress'.

"Some," said Catherine, "it seems have attained more 'progress' than others!"

1st August 1665

I fear for my soul, for on days such as today I have such ungrateful thoughts. Such thoughts I can express with my quill but would dare not share them with another. I have a feeling of resentment that dwells within me. A resentment of the fact that I am born a woman, though be it one of happy circumstance.

Imagine to bare grudge against the very thing that makes life possible. Yet what sits not easy in me is the lack of control we womenfolk are handed. Our chores start from the moment we arise and oft times, end not much afore it is the hour to retire. We have no bell marking the time we must work and the hours we might rest. Even for those men in the field who rise with the sun and work late into the evening, they might spend the hours left to them in leisure, drinking in the tavern, whilst we sit at home cleaning, mending or at our piece work. True we have not the strength nor stamina required of the men who work the mines but are not our hours at least equally long, with little or no financial recompense?

Even more unjust, it seems, is what we as women must tolerate. It is our unfortunate lot that we must endure silently a misguided union. Some I know suffer violence at the hand of their spouse; others despair as their husbands earnings are frittered away in 'The King's Head' or 'The Miners' Arms', whilst there are hungry mouths sat at table at home. Thank the Lord that Mother chose more wisely, for though Father has a temper and is not without fault, he is neither a savage nor a senseless man.

It seems to me that even those women who marry well are disadvantaged, for they are ever beholden to their husbands and must follow them in the life that they have chosen. Young, wealthy men, on the contrary, have the world at their feet. They may choose to travel, to set up in industry or even to study. The most women can hope for is that a caring, loving, wealthy man might chose her to marry.

I am fortunate in the fact that Rowland tolerates my passion for learning, though he does neither share nor understand it. I have told him that I, in turn, could teach him to be literate but he states that he does not have the inclination. His father, he points out, has managed thus far by appointing someone to correspond on his behalf and he intends to do the same. He did concede, however, that my being literate would be an advantage, for our interests for the business would correspond and there would not be the issue of lack of trust or delays due to absence. I would happily take on such a role but alas, I could not be seen to do so; after all, this is not work for a woman.

I am not bemoaning my state, for I am made most aware of my good fortune in my relationship with Rowland and my position at the rectory. It is the unjust nature of our destiny that berates me.

Catherine has said that it is a cruel trick of fate to bless a woman with intelligence, for oft times, it is not a blessing at all but rather a curse, for it leads only to frustration and disillusion. I believe she may speak reason. Were I of a less reflective nature, I may well have been whistling, humming or even singing as I scrubbed the stairs this day rather than suffer being possessed by such an ill-temper!

3rd August 1665

Today we all attended the marriage of Edythe Carter to Edward Taylor, it being three weeks almost to the day since their hand-fasting at the rectory. Elizabeth was verily in a state of great excitement and agitation induced by her role of bridesmaid. This morning, after her bathing, I tied some lengths of rag into her still damp hair and helped her into one of Mother's best gowns that we had altered slightly for the occasion.

With her large, brown eyes and her silken, black hair that shines like the feathers of a well-preened crow in the sunlight, Elizabeth's beauty has oft been remarked upon. Indeed, she has never a shortage of possible suitors vying for her attentions. Still, as she descended the stairs, her hair hanging in full ringlets and her cheeks pinched pink, we were all momentarily rendered speechless by the vision before us. For a vision she indeed was. The fern-green dress of Mother's hung perfectly from her statuesque form, accentuating the firm roundness of her breasts, her slim waist and the perfect contour of her hips. This surely was not our Elizabeth that stood before us but rather some female deity.

On passing us she smiled and her soft eyes sparkled with anticipation.

"Come now, or we shall find ourselves to be tardy."

It was with these words that our vision glided out of the door, the rest of us following in awe. I, for my part, feeling not a little shamed at the suddenly apparent plainness of my own appearance, it seeming a good deal less than adequate by comparison.

The sun at its zenith shone down upon the foregathered congregation who, like a trail of obedient ants, dutifully made their way from the bottleneck at the church gates and up the narrow yet well-trodden, grass pathway that led to the entryway. The large, wooden door having been propped wide open, gaped the darkness from within.

The interior was a deliciously cool haven from the parching heat outside of its walls. Catherine had installed some arrangements of flowers plucked from her garden. A large bunch stood at the foot of the alter and two smaller bouquets sat either side of the aisle against the front row of pews. Edward waited nervously, alternating his weight from one foot to the other. A fine figure of a man he cut, attired so in his doublet, breeches and hose. The hem of his long cloak brushed the tops of his newly polished boots.

Edythe and her father, Mr. Carter, led the small wedding procession, followed by Elizabeth and Bridget Talbot, her bridesmaids. Bridget looked girlishly pretty in her autumnal orange gown with yellow flowers pinned to its front and matching ones forming a crown in her auburn hair. However, it had to be admitted that she was overshadowed by Elizabeth in all her splendour. As I am sorry to state, was the bride. Fortunately Edythe was not one to take umbrage, she being too sensible in persuasion to be concerned by trivialities such as vanity.

The vows having been exchanged, all headed back to the bride's family home, led jovially by a small band of musicians hired especially for the occasion from the town of Bakewell. Their jaunty renditions continued whilst in the large back garden, the guests merrily toasted the newlyweds. After only a few hours most of the women folk, used to drinking less than their male counterparts, became quite animated, due no doubt to the intoxicating mixture of the uncommon heat and the alcohol. As the evening light grew ever more sombre, candles were lit and placed upon the tables. Mother and Father had already departed taking Joseph, Alice and Richard with them. Ellen and Sarah left a little later. As the night wore on, the remaining crowd drowsily dispersed, 'til only a handful of us remained. I had stayed beyond my preferred hour of departure in order to safely accompany Elizabeth home, for she had become quite dizzy with drink and her laughter was oft heard above the chattering of the remaining guests.

After persistent encouragement, I eventually managed to persuade Elizabeth to bid her farewells and proceeded to tentatively steer her towards the front of the house and out of the garden gate. I could not help but notice on thanking Edythe for such a wonderful day and giving her my own best wishes, that her eyes were red-rimmed as if she had been crying. I assumed at the time that it was from tears shed through either joy or emotion; however, I was to learn from Elizabeth on our journey homeward that this was indeed not the case.

"I quite simply cannot tolerate that self-righteous old hag... You know Emmott, she forbid Ann to be bridesmaid to Edythe... Indeed, she would not even allow her to attend the wedding... Indeed, she has insisted since the hand-fasting that Ann have no contact with her at all... And the two being so close for longer than anyone can remember. Poor Edythe was so upset and this was to be, so it is said, one of the happiest days of her life... And all ruined by that... by that... monstrous, heartless woman. By God... I wish she were here now... I would tell her exactly my thoughts upon the subject."

Never before had I heard Elizabeth so indignant, nor have I witnessed her to be so slighting of anyone's character. It was all quite contrary to her usual reasoned and balanced temperament. Yet, I have frequently noted that such anomalies occur. That the dark harbourings of the heart are oft let slip through alcohol drenched lip. Hence I rarely partake of such a pastime, for I would dread to think what deep secrets or shameful opinions might, without the censorship of reason or control, escape my own sweet mouth!

Elizabeth continued her rant until we reached the threshold. Thence I explained patiently that all would be asleep and that we must enter and retire in silence. Elizabeth placed one finger to her lips and began to utter, 'Sshh," and then stifle her giggles. With some difficulty, I helped her up the stairs and to our room, whereupon she dived upon her mattress and were it not that I had pulled her dress from her and removed her shoes, her giggling all the while, I do believe she would have slept fully clothed. By the time I had undressed and climbed into bed myself she had already begun to emit deep, resonating snores, much as Father does after an evening spent at 'The Miners' Arms'.

20th August 1665.

Mother, Elizabeth, Ellen and I spent the day scrubbing the house from top to bottom in preparation for the Wakes' celebrations. Father has already tended to the garden and we are all agreed that the whole house, both inside and out, is looking quite at its best. The children took to running around the house and garden, even the smallest have been infected by the excitement and anticipation that hangs in the air, though they possess no understanding of what its cause might be.

Having perspired so from toiling in the sweltering heat, before taking leave to meet Rowland, I filled the tub and washed myself down. Feeling thus refreshed, I made my way to The Cross where I saw him waiting for me in the shade of a tree. The village was verily a hive of activity. Womenfolk sat in the shade of doorways making garlands and many of the men folk, not employed this day in the mines, had taken to whitewashing their houses or repairing broken fences.

The streets were full of our neighbours and their visitors who had made the journey especially for the festivities and were now proudly being shown around the village. I declared to Rowland that I had never before seen the village so full of people, to which he replied it was no doubt due to the exceptionally fine weather we had been enjoying these last months. With more people surely still to arrive and the miners given leave to partake of the festivities, I do believe the village will be nigh on bursting come St. Helen's Day.

As we traversed The Cross, we overheard the men debating on how best to organise the bull baiting for this year. Mr. Howe lurked silently in the background as they stood about the large metal hook secured to the floor, to which the wretched creature was to be chained. There, the dogs, which appear as if frenzied by fever, are set loose to hound and torment the poor beast, which if managing to escape death, is left horribly injured and maimed. It is told that the meat of a baited bull is indeed more tender, though I cannot imagine why. Luckily, Rowland and I both agree the sport to be cruel and decided we would avoid bearing witness to such a ghastly scene. How fortunate I consider myself in having a man of a gentle nature, who is not turned violent or idiotic by alcohol, nor is he prone to betting and frittering away his hard-earned wages on such a vile spectacle.

On reaching the village periphery we commented on how scenic it looked this day. The gardens are full of flowers and summer vegetables sitting in neat rows. Lawns have been trimmed and bushes clipped and the house fronts, many already covered in variegated ivy, are decorated further with colourful garlands. So pretty was the scene in all directions that no artist would lack inspiration for their blank canvas.

We climbed the path that leads from the village to the boundary stone. The air felt warm and sweet and we could feel the sun's warmth on our faces. Sunlight dappled the woodland floor. The trees stood tall and verdant, ferns sheltered in the shadows of their twisted roots and scattered foxgloves attracted a fluttering of butterflies. We stopped a while, as if spellbound, to gaze at this charming scene. Clouds of midges danced vertically in the streams of sunlight and sounding above our beating hearts, the sky was full of birdsong. We exchanged smiles and squeezed hands in silent gratification. How full of joy I felt and how light of heart, my very soul felt bathed in beauty and love. I understood then, innately, what Catherine means when she talks of God being found in the nature which surrounds us.

We walked for a good few hours, chatting happily all the while. It was the ringing of the curfew bell that caused us to realise that the hour was tardier than we had imagined. The sun was low in the sky upon my return, and Ma chastised me gently for they all had already eaten; little matter, as I felt no hunger despite the long ramble. Later I sat with Mother, helping her with the spinning. Through the open windows we could hear the banging, shouting and merrymaking as the preparations continued. Together we talked and laughed and I marvelled at the youthful glow in her cheeks and the gleam in her eyes. Does she never tire?

A day nearer to perfection I strive to imagine! All is well!

28th August 1665

The Wakes' tide festival was a wonder to behold this year. Never have I witnessed so many people crammed into our small village. All talk is of the throngs of visitors and the great success of the festivities so enjoyed by all. Bodies spilled from both 'The Miners' Arms' and 'The Bold Rodney Inn' for nigh on two days. The air rang with shouts of mirth and laughter. Given that there were many who had imbibed of perhaps a little too much, the mood remained charitable and all seemed inclined more to goodwill than to offend. Indeed, I heard of no fights or skirmishes between revellers which is, I believe, quite unheard of. It is told of only one person receiving an injury during the celebrations. It appears that poor Unwinn was stepped on accidentally as he lay slumped in the tavern doorway, senseless from drink. Quite when the incident occurred and of the perpetrator no one can tell, for apparently he took rest there for the entire duration of the merrymaking!

There was, however, the incident at the church during divine service! Catherine believes it was a small group of young men from the next village, who, most probably encouraged by ale, ushered a young heifer into the church. The service was at once interrupted as all heads turned to discover the cause of the sudden commotion. The animal was set upon immediately by the dog whippers. The congregation then watched in some dismay as the wardens, in their confusion, unwittingly drove the poor beast towards the alter. It being confused itself, and without doubt panicked and frightened, proceeded to defecate. I noticed at this point that a few of the ladies who were unfortunate enough to be standing in the foremost pews before the alter, had begun to turn quite pale. Indeed, Mrs. Bagshaw started to swoon and had to be supported by her daughter, Ann, who all of a fluster herself, tried in vain to revive her by violently flapping her kerchief at the poor afflicted woman's face.

Thanks be that the dog whippers, they, having by this time recovered from the initial shock, managed to organise themselves and thereby succeeded in rounding up the animal and so shepherded it towards the arched doorway; that being the direction from whence it had appeared. Once we were settled and Mrs.

Bagshaw quite recovered, Mr. Mompesson continued the service whilst the wardens tried to subtly remove the remains of the foul deposits. They could not however eradicate the vulgar stench that persisted, which it must be said, detracted somewhat from the rest of the sermon.

Indeed, it was the incident of the young heifer that dominated most of the conversation that afternoon rather than the service itself. Such an occurrence had caused shock and dismay amongst the congregation, some of whom talked of the divine retribution that may befall us all, for such a sacrilegious act. This was done naturally out of earshot of the reverend who has no patience for such 'superstitions'. Luckily there were other distractions enough that afternoon and evening to dispel somewhat the memory and re-telling of this unfortunate event.

This afternoon Rowland and I watched the goose riding. The dead goose had been tethered by the feet and hung from a line which stretched across the street and was attached at each end to a house front. It was mainly the young men from Eyam and the surrounding local villages that partook of the sport. Quite a lot of strength and coordination is needed to steer the horse under the goose so that one is able to grab its neck to tug upon. After the best part of an hour had passed, the poor goose had a neck nigh on twice as long as is naturally given. It was Mr. Hadfield, from the cottage across from ours, who finally severed the head and won the goose for himself. A great cheer broke out from the local residents and those who had placed wagers on his success congratulated themselves.

Rowland's uncle was entering his finest cockerel in one of the fights on the green, so we meandered through the crowds and made our way to the top of the village. Arm in arm we were, for fear of being separated. Occasionally we stopped to greet friends, neighbours or relatives, or to peruse some of the stalls, so that the journey took at least thrice times as long as it would on any other day.

On the far side of the green, a small circular clearing had been made and walled by some old hay bales. Sawdust had been scattered therein upon the ground. Around this were already crowded a large group of folk. From their midst came shrill, clucking sounds, the ruffling of feathers and scratching of claws. The tournament had already begun. Rowland and I slowly made our way through the throng until we found a vantage point for ourselves.

I watched as two large cockerels pecked at and butted one another, tearing at each other's plumage and flesh until the blood began to trickle from their wounds. I was impressed by the ferocity with which they fought, no rules, no control, just a thirst for blood and instinct to harm. After a good half-hour of battling, one of the birds seemed to be now weakening, its opponent quick to sense this and with the encouragement of the crowd, began to attack anew and with more violence than before. The weaker bird suddenly submitted to defeat. Its thin legs crumpled, propelling its torso forwards upon the ground. It rested momentarily in this position, motionless. Its breathing was heavy. Its chest heaved, emitting a horrible rasping sound. In an instant, its neck fell sideways followed by the rest of its body. The victor continued to peck intermittently and with some disinterest at the now limp bunch of feathers before it, which lay brown and thickly clumped in the congealed blood. The same feathers, that only a short while before, were a magnificent display of velveteen colour, shining as the evening sunlight was caught upon them.

The victor eventually turned its back on the lifeless heap that lay prostrate before it. Distracted and made newly afraid by the shouts and cries of the onlookers, it began to dart from one side of the circle to the other. Now desperately, with its wings flapping, it mustered all of its remaining energy in a bid to escape. At this point, the proud owner, Rowland's uncle, stepped into the ring and gathered the terrified creature into his arms. The cries of the crowd reached a crescendo as the bird was held aloft. Meanwhile, the eyes of the vanquished stared vacantly into the sun. Its beak was still agape where it had attempted to draw its last breath or maybe release its last cry of agony. As the crowd abated and gradually drifted away, the winning bird was carried out of the ring. Only when it was placed back into its basket did it let down its guard and slump exhausted against the wicker restraints. Its head was bleeding from one side, its chest rising and falling in an exaggerated fashion.

As we left, two more baskets were being carried into the centre of the ring and wagers were being placed. A bird stood proudly in each container. One preened itself, gently caressing its silken feathers. The other pecked at the wooden lattice that imprisoned it. It was sobering to think that one of these creatures, in the prime of life, would soon be joining the bodies of the vanquished, already forgotten and slung carelessly to one side. There left to the mercy of the flies as they festered in the warmth of the descending sun. How glad I was that they were yet in happy ignorance as to their fate, knowing not that for one of them, the ties to this life were soon to be so hastily and violently severed. Proving true, what oft times I have heard said, that our ignorance as to our fate is indeed a blessing. What strange creatures men are, to enjoy such sports that bring the sights and smells of death to such a joyous occasion.

As the sun set, music could be heard above the noise of the throng and the dancing began. A band made up of members of the various local villages played with both vigour and talent. Elizabeth, who loves to dance, partnered with her close friend Elizabeth Blackwell, skipped in happy circles. Mary and Bridget Talbot, being slightly more modest in nature stood to their side, clapping enthusiastically. Before long the green was full of happy revellers, skipping and twirling to the rhythm of the band and the night air filled with shouts and laughter.

Mr. Morten had slaughtered one of his suckling pigs from Shepherd's Flatt and it was now roasting on a spit above the fire pit. Mrs. Morten stood aside him, their children about her legs. The pig's trotters had been bound together and a wooden pole crudely inserted into its rectum, the pole exited through the poor beast's mouth. It is oft told by old Mr. Marsh, who tried in vain to rescue the two young girls, Emily and Sarah, from the fire of 1629 that razed 'The King's Head', that roasting pig flesh has the same odour as that of burning human flesh. I cannot halt this frightful notion from coming to mind whenever the smell of a hog roast prevails in my nostrils.

As I turned my back on the sight, Rowland took my hands in his and we danced merrily and energetically, smiling all the while into each other's eyes. We danced for a good hour or more so that we finally retired to sit upon a hay bale, red-cheeked and breathless. Rowland then did something that both surprised and delighted me greatly. From his trouser pocket he produced a clean, cotton handkerchief. Looking straight into my eyes he unwrapped it before me revealing a simple band of silver and said, quite simply, "Emmott, be mine."

Still breathless from the dancing and now made more so from shock, I could do nothing in response but fling my arms around his neck and whisper the word 'Yes', dryly into his ear. Upon which his features, hitherto set in earnestness, broke into the most radiant of smiles I have ever seen. We clung to each other then and laughed in delight.

So it is that we are to be married a year from now at the next Wakes' tide!

So it is that I, Emmott Sydall, am now secretly betrothed!

31st August 1665

It has been the most wonderful of summers. The weather has leant itself to many a trip to the delf, the brooks and forest. After chores, Catherine and I have spent many a pleasant afternoon with the children. As they have amused themselves, the two of us have taken shade beneath the canopy of a tree or sat upon a blanket on the hillsides, talking and studying together.

Rowland, my betrothed in all but ceremony, and I have met as many a time as opportunity has allowed us. We have decided to tell no one of our engagement until the New Year as his father is expected then to formerly hand the running of the mill over to his eldest son. What happy times the two of us have shared, walking the hills and valleys that surround the village. Oft times I have reflected on how lucky we are to live in such a place of beauty, equalled, I am sure, by few others.

The evenings have been long and mild so Elizabeth, Ellen, Mother and I have taken to doing our piece work in the garden or out the front. How less tedious the work seems for sitting out under the last rays of sun. We stitch and chatter happily until dusk, then, on the tolling of the curfew bell, our eyes already straining, we gather up our work and are forced to retreat inside. I write this now in the garden, leant against the old stone wall. The heat radiates from the sun-baked rock and penetrates my body from behind whilst my face is bathed in a warm, golden light.

Autumn is nearly upon us now. How I will miss these long summer days and evenings spent out of doors. It pleases me little to think of the evenings drawing in, them spent warming ourselves aside the hearth, the younger children fidgety and in need of entertainment. Us at our piece work, huddled around the oil lamps, our fingers made clumsy by the cold, and Father ill-tempered through fatigue, berating the children for their noise. Sarah tries to find ways to amuse them so they are occupied and hence refrain from any bickering that might otherwise ensue between them. More importantly, it keeps them from getting under Father's feet who, at this time of the day, has little patience or compassion left for anyone. An hour or so after supper and the children are ushered to their rooms where Ellen, Elizabeth or I will try our best to settle them for the night. Alice is always in need of a story and being afraid of the dark, is the last to find sleep. Indeed, an oil lamp is left on low in the room until our work is finished and we too retire wearily to bed.

These summer evenings when the children are able to play in the street and little Joseph gurgles happily, looking up into the branches of a tree, endlessly fascinated it seems by the movement of the leaves in the breeze, Father is of much better humour. He will even, at times, sit with us womenfolk and listen to our chatter a while. 'Tis a shame I feel that one of us elder girls were not born a boy for he hankers after, I believe, the company of an adult son. Richard, being only eleven years old, is of too young an age still to be of any real interest to him, his wayward behaviour being more a source of annoyance than of consolation.

The sun has set now and the light dims. The swallows have all settled for the night and no longer soar upon the warm streams of air, gorging themselves upon the multitude of insects found there. How perfect is this world made! How wonderful it is to be witness to it!

8th September 1665

Today the church bell rang to pronounce the funeral of Mr. Viccars. Catherine tells me that he was laid to rest in a far corner of the graveyard.

Being a journeyman and having no family present, he was not attributed a headstone, poor soul. All talk in the village is of his demise, it being so sudden and violent in nature. There are rumours of it being the pestilence but no one is sure whether this be truth or falsehood. If it were the plague, it is confirmed that he could not have bought it with him to the village, as he has been working for Mr. Hadfield, the tailor, for nigh on two months already. It is said the disease cannot be harboured dormant for such a length of time.

It seems that Mr. Hadfield and his wife Mary, who lodged the deceased, were overheard in conversation. Mr Hadfield, it is told, ordered a box from London. The box contained several bolts of cloth, some remnants and some pieces of second-hand clothing. Mr. Hadfield, being away on business when the box was to be delivered, left instruction with Mr. Viccars to open it upon arrival. The story goes that on opening the box, Mr. Viccars found the contents to be damp so shook them out and hung them before the fire to dry, and it was very shortly after this that he fell afflicted.

Everywhere in the village, talk is heard of how to recognise the tell-tale signs of those visited by plague. Of how to safeguard against it by means of prayers and amulets, and indeed the numerous remedies that may be procured, the strangest of which I have heard involves the sitting of a live chicken, pigeon or toad upon the swellings known as 'buboes'. It is said the creature then draws out the infection into its own body and on so doing, perishes or bursts! The sufferer has fair chance of recovery if the treatment is repeated and the creature fails to expire, for this, it is said, is sign that the toxin has been thus removed.

Whilst polishing the silver, Catherine sat by me listening as I recounted all I had heard, for she is not privy to the gossip of the streets. The poor soul grew paler by the minute. When I had finished relating all I knew, she simply made the sign of the cross and uttered in a whisper, "Dear God preserve us." Unusually the silver was completed in silence, her being quite affected by my news and I sensing she wished to hear no more on the matter.

I myself am afeared. We are all.

15th September 1665

Catherine, Elizabeth, Ellen and I took the younger children blackberry picking today. Armed with a variety of containers acquired from the rectory kitchen we paraded through the churchyard and out to the fields beyond, where we knew the hedgerows to be abundant with fruit. I perceived a slight shiver run down Catherine's spine as her pace quickened on passing the freshly dug grave of poor Mr. Viccars. She made the sign of the cross and under her breath I heard her whisper, "May God have mercy." Fortunately, the children were otherwise engaged and by them, the new mound of earth went unnoticed, hence needing no explanation.

Although not possessing the shortest of legs of those amongst us, Alice complained of the climb. Sarah, as sweet-natured and patient as ever, comforted her and told her stories so that she might be distracted from the ascent. Elizabeth and Ellen took turns in carrying the smaller children on their backs, much to the little one's delight, who shouted encouragement and kicked hard with their heels as though they were riding a pony.

Eventually we came to the hedge at the far side of the field. It was full of hawkweed, bindweed and the last of the season's cranesbills. Elizabeth and Ellen being the eldest headed to the far corners, deep in whispered conversation and stifled giggles, as always. Richard and George hovered close to Catherine and I, being forewarned that there would be severe consequences if they attempted to run off and disappear, as was their wont. Little Elizabeth clung to her mother's skirts whilst Sarah paired off with Alice who was still engrossed in the tale of the poor orphan girl's search for her long-lost sister, who it seems, due to her unequivocal beauty, had married a very wealthy and handsome nobleman!

The children happily picked the blackberries from the hedgerow, holding aloft with a gleeful shout the biggest and juiciest for all to see. From the stains around their mouths and upon their fingers, I think it was fair to say that almost as many were eaten as were collected. All were gainfully occupied in this pursuit for a good hour or more, the hedgerows being so plentiful, that our baskets, pots and bowls were soon near to full. Indeed, we were just on the verge of regrouping and retreating when the air was pierced by a shrill scream. We all recognised it at once to be that of Alice, it having been heard oft times before.

Alice had sunk to the ground and sat holding her thumb aloft. Sarah already had her arm around her sister's shoulder and was doing her best to console her. Catherine and I rapidly and carelessly placed our baskets upon the ground and hurried over. On closer inspection we could see that Alice was quite beside herself, tears ran in rivulets down her cheeks and her complexion was markedly paler in shade than normal. The cause was apparent, for from the thumb she held aloft ran a trickle of bright, red blood which had begun to drip and collect in the lap of her skirt, forming a deep, crimson stain which crept ever further as it bled at the edges. From a very early age, Alice had always had a strong aversion to blood, the sight of which rendered her quite hysterical. By the time Catherine and I were at her side Sarah, being of a more practical nature, had managed to wrap her kerchief tightly around the injured thumb and had so stemmed the flow of blood.

Richard and George, used to such outbursts from Alice, had been quite nonchalant about the whole affair and had calmly installed themselves beside the abandoned baskets and were happily devouring their contents. After a long hug and many noises and words of consolation, Alice eventually managed to calm herself and recovered sufficiently, so as to be able to follow the rest of us back to the rectory, all be it sniffling all the way. It was only upon Catherine producing some bread and honey from the kitchen larder that Alice's misery was finally abated.

Whilst the younger children amused one another and ate, the eldest retreated to the garden to continue their sharing of village news, unhindered and uninterrupted. Catherine and I meanwhile made some pastry which we then rolled into thin sheets in readiness to bake some blackberry pies. The remainder of the fruit we placed in a large pot to which we added a little sugar and water. It was left upon the hearth until it began to bubble laboriously, exploding thick purple blemishes onto the sides of the pan. This we would leave to cool, to later bottle for preserve to be spread upon bread.

By the time we had cleared away it was well passed lunchtime. Carrying two of the blackberry pies, I rounded the family up and we set off for home. Mother set the pies out upon the supper table this same evening and we all agreed how much better they tasted for having picked the fruit ourselves. Even Alice was greatly cheered and seemed to have forgotten the unfortunate occurrence of that morning, especially when father declared that it was the best blackberry pie he had ever tasted! Catherine and I will bottle the preserve tomorrow.

20th September 1665

Talk of the plague had all but subsided, it being ten days since the interment of the unfortunate Mr. Viccars. Today, however, it has recommenced in earnest as little Edward Cooper, Mary Hadfield's son from her former marriage, has been taken with a violent fever. The physician, Humphrey Merril, has attended and it is rumoured that the poor mite complains of heaviness of limb, a raging thirst and nausea, all of which are known symptoms of the pestilence.

Having finished my chores at the Mompessons', Rowland and I walked upon the hills this afternoon. Rowland tells me that news of Eyam's possible visitation has reached Stoney Middleton and other surrounding villages. There is some panic and even talk from some anxious inhabitants of putting guards at their boundaries to prevent any person from Eyam entering.

"Fret not Emmott, for they will not keep me from thee," he assured me, squeezing the hand he clasped. "For how would I fare then?"

It was a fine afternoon up on the mount. The light, being now autumn soft, made giant bedclothes of the rolling hillocks and cotton balls of the sheep. The sun still has some warmth to it and the air is mild yet. Even so, I noted the leaves starting to turn on the trees and the branches begin to hang heavy with fruit. A few final brave swallows still drift on the temperate breeze, feasting upon the small insects taking evening flight.

On my return to the house, I heard such dreadful utterances emitting from the Hadfield's cottage opposite. From the opened upstairs window came forth cries so doleful that they sent a shiver up my spine and made the hairs upon my body erect, so as to prickle my skin. Indeed, they sounded barely human and more resembled the sounds of a beast at slaughter. I hurried inside and hastily shut the door upon them.

In my head, as I sit here and write, I can hear them still. I fear they will haunt my dreams tonight. God bless us all.

23rd September 1665

The church bells tolled again today as we were called upon to pay our last respects to young Edward who passed yesterday. Most of the villagers were present, many for genuine reasons, some, it must be said, more through curiosity. Mrs. Hawkesworth was noticeable in her absence for it is said she stayed at home to nurse her son Peter, who is now also stricken with the distemper. There is little doubt now that it is indeed the plague that we are cursed with. There was fear and anxiety plain to see in the faces of those gathered at church today. People no longer talk in excited exaggeration of the pestilence but rather in whispers, huddled in corners, as if the disease itself had ears that might hear them. I noticed today several villagers with amulets about their person. I have heard tell that Mr. Talbot, the smithy, is through demand forging copies of the talisman most favoured by the inhabitants of those other municipalities who share in our unfortunate fate. Those who wear the cross of Christ around their neck, I have remarked, reach for it with much increased regularity. I am sure that all, like myself, are praying a little more frequently and fervently.

At the service today Mr. Mompesson was seen to be walking with a limp. This afternoon, whilst preparing the potage at the rectory, I made comment of this to Catherine, thinking he must somehow have afforded himself an injury. On the mention of it, Catherine burst into sobs revealing that she had observed a green ichor issuing from an inexplicable wound upon his leg and was convinced it was a sign of the plague. Placing my arms around her I did all in my power to alleviate her of her anxieties. I remarked that he bore no fever, no nausea or bodily aches and that indeed, apart from the infection in his leg, he was of sound health. My words did appear to calm her somewhat; she sat a while then and practised upon her clavichord whilst I listened, lost in quiet contemplation. By the time it was for me to take my leave, she seemed much recovered and quite herself again.

This evening we attended the Arthel dinner for little Edward. It was indeed a solemn affair. Poor Mary was quite beside herself with grief. I had no appetite for the biscuits given, as is customary, on our departure.

On our return there was a sudden squall in the gentle breeze which sent myriads of leaves gently tumbling to the ground.

25th September 1665

Our Sarah is taken to bed with fever. We all pray that it is but a common ailment but silently we fear the worst. She asks for water constantly and no matter how much we fetch her, she seems unable to quench her raging thirst. She shivers and complains of coldness but from her body comes a heat that burns like hot coals. She is too tired of body to move herself, so Mother and I must help her to the bathroom. We nurse her without sharing our concerns. No one dare utter the word that occupies all our minds, as if in doing so the foul beast might be unleashed. If it be that which we so dread, we will know soon enough for it attacks swiftly and with much violence, a week at most is all the body can endure.

My hand shakes now as I write this. Mother is quietly hysterical; she summoned me but an hour or so ago. By the hand she led me to Sarah's bedside. On pulling back the bedclothes and lifting her arm, she solemnly indicated a lump the size of a small egg under her right armpit. The lump was livid and lead-coloured with a blackish spot in the centre. It must have manifested itself quite recently, for it was not there this afternoon when I wiped her over with a wet cloth. Our eyes met in despair and disbelief as she re-covered Sarah, who had already began to complain of the cold.

In the hallway, out of earshot, we embraced and talked in hushed voices of what must best be done. We determined to tell Father but not the younger children who were already settled in their beds, for fear of alarming them. They are all to be kept clear of the room. We laid beds for Elizabeth and Ellen in the parlour and Father has left already to seek out Humphrey Merrill, the physician, and the Reverend for advice. Mother is at Sarah's side, mopping her brow and refilling her glass.

Since the initial panic and misery, a quiet dread has settled throughout the house. Oh Lord protect us. I doubt any of us will find repose this night. What will become of us?

Mrs. Hawkesworth's son, Peter, was buried yesterday.

26th September 1665

Sarah is worse today. She refuses to take anything; the mere sight of food initiates a sort of fit of anxiety. She has taken to vomiting regularly. As fast as Mother and I clean her she begins again. She falls in and out of sleep but her dreams are troubled, she mutters, rambles and moans and cannot seem to find rest. At night I wrap the pillow around my ears and pray to sleep, so I might not hear the pitiful wails and cries that tug so upon my heart strings.

The buboes that are upon her seem to cause her unrelenting distress. She has one still under her arm and another has appeared beneath her right ear. We dress and care for them as best we can. Catherine called today with a poultice she had prepared which we duly applied but still they do not break. She suffers dreadful sores around her lips and nostrils and purple blotches have appeared upon her skin. The room is filled with the vile stench of her infection so that we must continually leave the windows open.

Catherine tells us that both Thomas and young Mary Thorpe next door are also taken with the distemper. Mother went to visit Mary this evening and took her some of the broth I had made. On her return, I did not ask her how they fared, for her countenance was so heavy with pain and misery that there was not need. I no longer pray for Sarah's recovery but rather that she find peace. That You might take her hand and this hellish suffering be done.

27th September 1665

Thomas passed yesterday. Mother insisted on going to the funeral; her and Mrs. Thorpe being more like sisters than friends. Father was at the mines so Ellen accompanied her. They prepared hastily and without fuss. I stayed and cared for Sarah and little Joseph. The funeral was a short affair for they were back within an hour. There was no gathering after as young Mary is afflicted badly.

Sarah is quieter today. It seems she has trouble drawing air and her voice is but a dry whisper. She is too weak to scream or cry; instead she releases a soft, doleful whimpering like that of a dying animal. At times she takes reprieve in a deep and death-like sleep from which there is no stirring her. She passes much liquid and blood from her bowels and bladder, the stench from which is vile and quite overpowering. Her stomach is now enormously distended and her skin appears blue in colour. Occasionally, her whole body convulses and she momentarily opens her eyes, but they are unseeing and roll into the back of her head. Her features become distorted in agony so that she is barely recognisable. It is as if her soul is already elsewhere. What kind of a disease is this that savages the body so? An uglier one I have neither seen nor heard of.

Mother knows that Sarah is dying. She cares for her now as she would a newborn baby; with a tenderness that acknowledges the battle to be already lost. Father comes in from time to time and hovers in the doorway, shifting his weight from one leg to the other whilst looking on helplessly. The younger children are kept away as agreed, for this is no sight for their innocent eyes.

30th September 1665

Dear Sarah is at peace at last. She is the fifth victim of this illness. The house is strangely quiet. Mother rocks in her chair. I know not how to comfort her. I keep house and Father prevents the younger children from misbehaving but they are subdued anyway and need little correcting.

My poor, sweet Sarah. How I long to hear that constant chattering and giggling that before I found so tiring. Her life has ended so quickly and horribly, yet less than a month ago we could not have dreamt such a thing could come to pass. The plague is sweeping through our village and has now claimed one of ours as its latest victim.

The Banes are also visited. The shadow of death hangs over each and every one of us like a cloud of dread, shading the whole village. It is random in its path and there is no logic or sense to it. Our only defence is prayer, yet that does not keep it at bay. Life suddenly seems like the most fragile string of pearls which might at any time be broken; past and future dropping to the floor and rolling away.

It is supposed best, on advice of the physician, that we dispose of the bedclothes and night attire. Father has already placed them outside the back door in a pathetic bundle. The body was removed quickly after death. I am ashamed to say it but I was eager to clear the room. I cannot describe the stench that has lingered these past days, so thickly vile that you might choke upon it. The windows now lie wide open and we have burnt candles and fistfuls of lavender and rosemary in an attempt to disguise the putrid air.

Mrs. Thorpe is now downstairs with Mother, young Mary passed this evening. I fear they are of little comfort to one another, being both so raw with grief. How strange to think it was not so long ago that they were remonstrating over the matter of a stone wall. How quickly such animosities sink to oblivion in the face of disaster.

Dear Lord, protect us from this cruel disease that, in so short a time, horrifically transforms the beautiful, young and healthy into a pale and frightful shell of bone and stinking flesh. I remember my dear Sarah now, not as she was at the end, but as she is with You Lord, restored to her true self with soft curls, sparkling, brown eyes and cheeks slightly reddened in healthy glow.

Keep her close in your care Lord. We do miss her so.

May God bless also: George Viccars, Edward Cooper, Peter Hawkesworth, Thomas Thorpe, Mary Thorpe.

1st October 1665

We prepared solemnly for Sarah's funeral. Father polished our shoes whilst Mother bathed each of the little ones in turn. Only after dressing them and brushing through their hair did she turn her attention to her own preparations. As she started up the stairs, I saw Father put a comforting hand upon her shoulder. Mother acknowledged the gesture, placing her hand over his, then stifling her emotion she hurried up to her room.

Mother is a woman used to hardship and no stranger to grief, witnessing the loss of three of her siblings in their infancy and suffering her own mother's passing at the age of fourteen. Forgoing the selfishness of youth, she took it upon herself to raise her four younger brothers and sisters, so replacing their mother in her maternal duties. No wonder then that my grandfather, who never remarried, held a special place in his heart for his eldest child. He would often say of her that she had the head of a woman twice her years, the strength of an ox and the heart of an angel.

Mother descended the stairs as the passing bell began its weary toll. Upon the sound she faltered a little, her hand gripped the wooden rail a little more tightly so that her knuckles protruded and whitened. Almost immediately her back straightened, her chin raised an inch or so and with great composure she finished her descent and began to usher the children out of the front door. Rowland was stood respectfully awaiting our exit. He nodded gravely to my parents and then linked his arm in mine and we made our way to the front of the procession which had come to a halt before our door.

As we dolefully made our short journey to the church, the young girls of the village scattered flowers and herbs before us as is the custom. I recognised them all of course and tried to catch their eye, to acknowledge them and show my gratitude, but their pale faces were hung low and their gaze was fixed steadfastly to the ground. Elizabeth Blackwell and Mary and Bridget Talbot carried the virgin garlands at the front of the cortège, the three being Sarah's closest friends. The poor wretched creatures sniffled miserably for the journey's duration and continued to do so throughout the entire service. When it was time to hand over the virgin garlands to the attending wardens, so that they might be hung from the church rafters, Elizabeth began to sob quite uncontrollably and no consolatory words from Bridget or Mary seemed able to stem her flood of tears.

The service itself was noticeably shorter than customary and the interment brief but efficient, for the whole procedure was to be repeated later that day for young Mary Thorpe. Mr. Mompesson was, as always, sincere in his condolences and eloquent in speech. He spoke of death not as an end but rather a 'transformation'. I was grateful indeed that it was he leading the mourning. In his words I found some comfort. Catherine too was there and approached me at the graveside, offering sweet words of condolence whispered with heartfelt pathos.

It being a mild September we had arranged for the wake to be held in the garden. A handful of neighbours and friends made a brief appearance and then departed as soon as was possible without it being considered impolite. Mary stayed to the end bless her, even though she was to bury her own daughter in a matter of hours. That evening I criticised their behaviour. Mother, however, was quick to admonish me declaring that it was entirely understandable given the circumstances and that their fear and obvious discomfort was natural and no different to how we would have reacted, even though we would like to think it otherwise. On reflection I knew her to have spoken true.

Mother and Ellen attended Mary's funeral this afternoon. I minded the youngsters and prepared a potage for supper. Rowland stayed to offer me comfort but we were all very low in spirit.

Mother declined anything to eat and retired directly upon her return. Elizabeth looked much older that evening. It was as if the young girl had been left at the graveside and a woman returned home in her place. The grief etched clearly upon her face.

2nd October 1665

Mother fares badly. We are all in a state of shock. In the early hours of this morning we were all awoken by urgent shouts and a frantic knocking on the door. Father duly went to see what the cause of the commotion might be and upon opening the door, found Mr. Thorpe in a terrible state. He was ushered inside and once calmed slightly, he proclaimed that Mrs. Thorpe was dead. By this time Mother, on recognising the voice, had risen and descended to investigate the cause of Mr. Thorpe's outburst. Elizabeth, Ellen and I joined them shortly after, in time to hear Mr. Thorpe recount how his wife, on mounting the stairs to retire, suddenly collapsed and perished upon the spot. The physician, Humphrey Merrill, had already been summoned and pronounced her dead. On further investigation she was noted to have the 'token' upon her chest; a large, purple blotch known to be the mark of the plague. Her body has already been taken. After an hour or so my father escorted Mr. Thorpe back home, by which time his brother had arrived and so he left the poor, distraught man in his company.

Today at the rectory, Catherine tells me that Matthew Banes has perished and that Margaret, his wife, is also afflicted. We are people familiar with death, many of our children are lost in infancy or childhood, but this pestilence that has descended upon our village is unparalleled by any disease anyone can recall.

On my way to the rectory those that I passed held fear and dread upon their faces, some crossed the street so as to avoid my path for they know we are visited, others nodded and hastily continued upon their way. The streets are unusually quiet. Children no longer gather to play but are persuaded instead to rest inside for fear of contagion. At the market house a wooden bowl filled with vinegar has been placed upon the table. We are to leave our payment for any provisions in the bowl and any coins due to us are also placed there. It is said that the vinegar cleanses the coins from the scourge which may lie upon them. Other traders, I am told, are doing similar.

Many villagers have stopped making their weekly journey to Tideswell Market as it has been rumoured that any person from Eyam is no longer welcome there and that guards have been placed at every entrance. Mr. and Mrs. Thornley tell of how they were shouted at and even had clods of earth thrown at them by some of the townsmen. Indeed, they were verily hounded out of the town and forced to return to Eyam empty-handed.

5th October 1665

We all try to maintain some normality amidst this chaos that engulfs us. Father goes to the mine each day. Mother has taken up her spinning and piece work again aided by Ellen, whilst Elizabeth cares for the smaller children. I make my daily journey to the rectory. The routine, I think, helps us to keep our minds from dwelling on the possible fate that threatens us all. It is good to spend some time out of the house and in a different environment, one unencumbered by grief and loss. Spending time with Catherine, I try to put aside for some hours that which has befallen us.

Today we put to storage some of the vegetables we had pickled last summer. As we ladled the mixture into the jars, Catherine talked of those families who have fled to escape the plague. I noticed only yesterday that the Sheldon's house lies abandoned. Apparently, Catherine tells me, the whole family fled in great haste to their alternative residence yesterday evening. They had not far to journey, it being sited on the other side of the hill above Eyam. What a droll picture she painted with her description of their flight.

Their procession of carriages and carts was, she declared, a rare sight, being over-packed with seemingly anything they could lay their hands upon. Household goods and provisions burst through the windows of the carriage so that the children were almost buried and barely perceivable. The noise as they flew through the village was apparently quite deafening, as the pots and pans which they had secured to the roof by a length of rope, clanked and clanged. Behind the two over-laden carriages, the servants made chase in the old cart, steered single-handedly by Old Tom the gamekeeper, his other hand being gainfully employed in keeping his cap upon his head. They all held poultry upon their laps and shared their seats with a couple of hunting dogs, several startled geese and a fully-grown goat. The hens flapped, the dogs barked and the goat bleated anxiously between its attempts to consume the tails of Old Tom's coat.

Such was her description that I encountered no hardship in picturing the scene in my mind's eye and on doing so found I was unable to stifle my amusement. On remarking my mirth, Catherine too began to laugh until we both became quite hysterical. It was only upon Mr. Mompesson's entry that we regained our composure and remembered all those lost to us. But how good it was to laugh and hear laughter again; it was as replenishing as it was wicked.

My sins were punished hundred fold on my arrival home, for Mother reported that both Father and Richard were taken to bed with fever.

9th October 1665

Oh Lord preserve us. Father, Richard and Ellen are all with distemper. Catherine nurses the children; I attend to Father and Mother runs betwixt the three.

The house seems to be full of their pitiful cries and moans, the air so foul that there is no escape from its stench within these walls. Richard and Father have been suffering two days since and dear Ellen succumbed in the night. Richard has a bubo the size of a plum upon his neck which tortures him so that he can find no comfort. It appears to be at a head. Catherine has applied poultice and cloth soaked in boiling water, but still it will not burst.

Father suffers mainly in silence but I can see the pain pronounced in the desperate look in his eyes, the contortion of his features and the blood vessels in his neck that rise blue and look as though they might, at any moment, break through the skin. I wipe his forehead with a cold flannel and serve him water which he gulps in greedy fits, most of it running from his mouth and pooling in soaked patches upon the bedclothes. At times he becomes delirious and talks with urgency, yet I can make no sense of his utterances.

This evening whilst not of sound mind he was persuaded to get up and make his way downstairs, whereupon he began to put on his boots as if to leave the house. Luckily, Rowland had arrived shortly prior to Father's decision to take flight and with the help of Catherine and Mother, we managed to bring him back to bed. Dreadful as it sounds, we have had to restrain Father for fear of him taking leave of us in the night. There is no way that Mother and I could contain him alone, for when gripped with this madness he has the strength of two men. I am ashamed to say that his countenance at such times frightens me terribly for he begins to produce froth in the corners of his mouth and his eyes have a frantic look as they roll uncontrollably in his head. I no longer recognise this being before me as my father but rather some wild and atrocious beast.

Mother has sent me just to rest, neither of us having slept the night previous. How can I find rest when those I love are suffering so? How can I deafen my ears to their pleading cries? How can I harden my heart to their dreadful plight?

We have laid an old mattress for Rowland in the parlour. It is agreed that he is to stay at the house tonight so that Mother too might benefit from some respite, if she is able, or at least have some company through the long night if not. Elizabeth will be at hand to tend to Father and to comfort the young ones less they be disturbed in the night and awake, confused and afraid. Rowland settled the little ones to their beds this night. He told Alice stories of adventures at sea so that her mind might take her to a place far from this wretched reality and steer her instead into welcome reverie. Poor Alice, she has become more withdrawn than ever. She barely utters a word now but looks on through the parting of her long fringe with solemnity, a permanent frown etched upon her young face. This evil scourge has caused the most innocent of this village to pay witness to such horrors that it has quite cruelly and emphatically stripped them of their childhood.

I find solace in the thought that Rowland and I are under the same roof, yet it does afford me some trouble too. I pray that the Lord will preserve him.

My eyes begin to fail me, my limbs have become heavy and my mind weary.

Keep us all safe in your arms good Lord.

12th October 1665.

Richard passed yesterday. Today, those of us that were able attended his funeral. Catherine bided at the house to nurse Ellen and Father. The funeral was a brief affair; services are now held at the graveside. Rowland stood between Mother and I throughout. He supported Mother at the elbow and gripped my hand tightly as I leant against him. We did not loiter. Once the coffin had been lowered and the first spadefuls of earth thrown noisily upon it, we turned and made our way back to the house where we knew Ellen and Father were to grow weaker by the hour.

As I approached the house I prayed silently and selfishly that we might not find them both to be in a wakeful state, their bodies convulsed by that raw physical agony, but rather at peace in that death-like sleep from which they wake not but are taken directly to the Lord's kingdom. Catherine greeted us at the threshold with condolences and news of the sick. Ellen, we were informed, lay still and restful but Father by contrast had become quite agitated. Rowland and I talked a while with Catherine in the parlour whilst Mother went to attend to Father.

Catherine told us that Mrs. Bagshaw and her daughter, in a bid to prevent infection, have taken to going about their business with a neckerchief tied around their heads so obscuring their nose and mouth. Apparently they visited the rectory to pay a call on Mr. Mompesson yesterday, sporting their new fashion. It seems that Mrs. Bagshaw, considering herself a devout Christian, takes it upon herself to pay the rector her respects at least three times a week, engaging him in discussion, at a safe distance of course, of her own understanding of certain passages in both the Old and New Testaments. This, despite the fact (and this was relayed by Catherine with that familiar and mischievous glint in her eye which I have come to know so well), that Mr. Mompesson has insisted that it really is quite unnecessary, and her time might be better spent serving the Lord and those afflicted in alternative activity.

Anyway, it seems that Mr. Mompesson need not suffer many more such visitations in the future, as Mrs. Bagshaw had called to lamentably inform him of her decision to take herself and her daughter Ann to the safety of relatives in Manchester. She did however enquire as to whether Mr. Mompesson might be so good as to find time between services and his visits to the sick and grieving to keep an eye on Bagshaw Hall, for she was convinced that the thought of it lying empty and unattended would afford her many a sleepless night. She was then so bold as to leave a key (not wanting to risk contamination through any kind of physical intimacy) upon the arm of a chair. Upon doing so she proceeded to explain that, of course, she trusted the rector implicitly and knew that she could be secure in the knowledge that her possessions would be found just as she had left them upon her return, at such a time when God saw fit to remove the dreadful scourge that had descended upon the village of Eyam. She had however, she continued to inform him, for her own peace of mind made quite an exhaustive itinerary of her belongings.

Catherine said she was unsure as to her husband's immediate reaction to this soliloquy, but it was telling that the key had been placed in an old cloth purse and pushed to the back of his desk drawer.

Rowland and I could not help but smile, for it is the subtlety of saying so much without saying anything untoward, that Catherine has mastered so well and it is just that which makes her company so amusing, even in the direst of circumstances. It is no wonder that all are drawn to her: the young, the old, the poor, the rich, the healthy and the sick. Being in her presence is like opening the window and breathing in the sweet spring air after having just before inhaled the sallow stench of disease. Both herself and her husband have, with their words and kindness and with no thought for their own well-being, brought to the dying upon transition and to the grieving, great peace and solace. Thanks be to God for sending us souls such as these. Thanks be to God for friends such as these.

Before supper, Rowland and Catherine took Joseph and Alice out for an hour or so, they took them for a walk up on the ridge. On their return they stayed a while as I finished preparing the potage. They told of 'pest houses' having been built up on the common land. Crude structures fashioned from wood, metal sheets and old tarpaulins by those who would rather take their chances against the ravages of winter, exposed on a hillside, than pit them against the plague here.

We ate supper in relative silence, our movements were sluggish, none of us having much of an appetite. In a bid to try and distract Mother a little, I related the story of the Bagshaw's, as we tidied the table and stacked the bowls. I tried to retell it as exactly as I could, for at any other time she would have been thoroughly amused by the whole incident. She nodded on a couple of occasions yet otherwise seemed barely to hear me.

15th October 1665

The house is strangely quiet once again. Father succumbed to the distemper yesterday evening and dear Ellen perished shortly after in the early hours of this morning. Today we are to bury them both. The misery I feel is no greater or lighter than yesterday for it is as if my mind and body have become insensitive to death and grief. I am as a cup that can only hold so much, before the contents spill over and are lost.

The passing bell rings out incessantly it seems and it is a sound now that we have come to accept with loathing. Catherine called at first light. She tells me that the rector at day's end will have buried sixteen since this merciless pestilence furtively crept in and took up home amongst us. Apparently, poor Mr. Mower, the carpenter, works both day and night in an attempt to supply the number of coffins required.

When will these horrors be at an end? How much more can and must we suffer?

Rowland came this morning to be greeted with yet more woeful tidings. He is to accompany Mother and I. What a strength he has been to us yet I fret for him so. If he too were to perish I would not have the will to go on, for I would care not whether the distemper were to consume me or not. What evil thoughts are these to entertain?

17th October 1665

I have been to the rectory today; I took Joseph and Alice with me. Mother remains quiet and subdued though continues with her piece work, Elizabeth at her side. It is more now, I am sure, to keep busy then to sell, for no one in the village is interested in buying such fare and there are no others to sell to. It would be a fool indeed who dared to cross the village boundary, unless it were of course, to visit loved ones. The weather has turned colder recently, so at the rectory the girls amused Joseph in front of the fire with some of Elizabeth's toys, taken from the nursery, whilst George played with his prized wooden boat, steering it precariously around the table legs.

Catherine and I sat at the other end of the room sorting the laundry. With the children out of earshot, Catherine confided in me that her heart is torn. Mr. Mompesson is urging her to take refuge with the children at the residence of his uncle, a Mr. John Bielby of Sheffield, whom, it is assured, will receive them gladly. Though fearful for Elizabeth and George, she insists her place is at her husband's side and so refuses to go. She is contemplating sending the children alone, but as yet has resisted the temptation to do so. Placing her hand upon mine, she turned to me and exclaimed,

"Oh Emmott, how could I look people like you in the eye. You who have lost so many of your loved ones, knowing that mine I have sent to safety?"

I replied, in no uncertain terms, that were anyone in this village offered such an opportunity they would not hesitate to take it. And they would surely not torture their souls with such feelings of guilt, so much relieved would they be to know their dearest were saved. Those of us that stay do so through no choice of our own, but because we are presented with no other option. Indeed, I urged her to reflect no longer and to speed her children and herself to this sanctuary afforded to them, before it were too late. At this instance our conversation was interrupted by Alice, who came to us in floods of tears.

It was ascertained, through stifled sobs, that little Elizabeth had so upset her by telling her that they could no longer play with the doll, as she had fallen ill with the pestilence. Catherine at once reddened through shame and anger and Elizabeth was severely reprimanded and spent the rest of the afternoon alone, in the nursery. I told Catherine not to be too harsh on her, for those so young in years and who have, thank the Lord, not witnessed at first hand the dreadful reality of their imaginings, can have no comprehension of such words and deeds.

On our return we found Mother quite panic stricken, for Elizabeth had taken to her bed feeling unwell. Mother is sure she is visited and upon observing her a while in her bed, I sadly had to admit agreement. I proceeded in trying to calm Mother for the sake of the other children.

Joseph and Alice are sleeping in with me this evening. Mother nurses Elizabeth. I have Rowland's ring clasped in my hand and will pray fervently for this horror to end.

20th October 1665

Alice is taken ill.

24th October 1665

Both Alice and Elizabeth have passed. I have not the heart to write nor words to express.

28th October 1665

I am thankful that neither Alice nor Elizabeth lingered long.

Poor, dear Alice had an enormous bubo under her jaw and another in her left armpit. The poultices we applied soothed them somewhat but did nowt to alter their size or appearance. Little Alice, always so quick to complain when ailing, did not vocalise her sufferings apart from the pitiful whimpering that accompanied her final hours; how peaceful she looked thereafter, as if she had merely drifted into some slumber to find but pleasant reverie.

Elizabeth also bore her demise with great courage. Indeed, she seemed more concerned for the welfare of others than for herself, as was her way in life. When sound of mind, she insisted all the while that she was in no great discomfort and would have neither Mother, nor myself, tend to her more than necessity demanded.

How disturbing it was for Mother and I, that during her last day on this earth our sweet-tempered and beautiful Elizabeth was transformed into something unrecognisable. The delirium rendered her offensive and her beautiful, large, brown eyes rolled uncontrollably in their orbs. Her usual high colour was replaced by a paleness, interrupted only by the blue veins that bulged in her neck during the spasms that afflicted her skeletal frame, and reduced her pretty features to the most awful of grimaces.

So it was, that both Mother and I shared a look of sad relief at her passing; for our mild-tempered beauty, had, before our very eyes, mutated into some being possessed.

Mr. Mower and Mr. Howe called that same day with the coffins for the girls. Mother remained in the parlour with Joseph, whilst I led them to the room where we had laid out their bodies. Mother and I had taken care in washing them and arranging their hair. We had dressed little Alice in her church-going clothes, and Elizabeth was attired in the fern green gown of Mother's that she had worn for Edythe's wedding. I could not help but remark inwardly upon the contrast of appearance of the then and now: the dream and the nightmare.

I could not watch and so averted my eyes, as their limp bodies, not so long ago so vibrant with life, were lifted into the crudely assembled wooden caskets and the lids duly, in turn, hammered down. Although irrational, I know, I couldn't help but fret over how alone and afraid they might feel.

The two men carried Elizabeth's body out first and after placing it upon the cart outside, returned for little Alice. So diminished were they at the end that it afforded the two strong men very little in the way of effort. The coffins, all being made aforehand and being of only one size - there being too many deceased to make each one to measure- were so not of correct length nor width for a small child. As Alice was taken down the stairs and rounded the corners, I could hear her body clattering around inside, like a lone walnut in a piggin. Mother placed her hand gently on each coffin in turn as they were passed through the parlour, loaded onto Mr. Howe's cart and driven away.

The funeral was a short, bleak affair. The October air was layered with mist and the pregnant, grey clouds that omitted their burden of a fine, continuous drizzle, hung low upon us. The sod was dark and claying and the thud it made as it hit the coffins, reverberated through our very flesh. Mother had insisted that the girls be buried together in a single grave. This practice has become quite commonplace, it being of mutual benefit to both the grieving and the sexton.

These are solemn days indeed. The very air seems to hang heavy with grief.

30th October 1665

How strangely large and eerily empty the house now seems with just myself, Mother and little Joseph. Thankfully, Joseph is too young to understand what has befallen us. Mother seems wasted with grief and is a mere shadow of the woman she was. She has abandoned her piece work and instead, having no care remaining for her own health, spends her days visiting the sick and dying. She sleeps now in the chair in the parlour. By morning, when I awake, she is usually already gone. Joseph and I leave the house for the vicarage shortly after. Like Mother, I can no longer bear the stillness and the silence, nor the sight in my mind's eye of when we were whole, children in all corners, the house filled with noise and movement so that you were hard pressed to find a quiet spot in which to retreat.

Rowland comes most days still; he meets me now at the rectory. He has become firm friends with Catherine and Mr. Mompesson, who shower us both with no end of kindness and words of comfort. Catherine always prepares more potage and bakes more bread than is necessary so that I might take some home for Mother and I for supper. After eating, Mother and I pass an hour or so in conversation, sharing news of the day or reminiscing of those better bygone days; days of normality, each glorious God-given one, taken quite for granted, happy in our ignorance of the horror, misery and heartache that in the blink of an eye was to be unleashed upon us.

It seems to me now that the structure of life is composed of opposites, contrasting states, and that we ride upon the pendulums that swing incessantly between them, oft times gently and other times violently thus reaching the extremes. We are all stuck upon these pendulums, powerless to the changing of their course, so that our only salvation is to pray to God to give us the strength we need to hold on and to have mercy upon us, so that we might once again swing more softly. So impressed was I with this reflection that I expressed these thoughts to Catherine, in the presence of Mr. Mompesson, this afternoon. I was surprised when it was he, not Catherine, who in turn addressed me; it is not his custom to enter into our discussions. He regarded me earnestly, yet his eyes were filled with gentleness and compassion. He then stated something I am not sure that I understand, but his conviction was so deep that the words are etched evermore upon my mind:

"All our thoughts, words and actions create our reality Emmott. We are never helpless, just unaware. Have faith in these dark and terrible times that there is reason to it, though we may see it not. Envisage and speak of constantly that which you wish for yourself and for us all, for together we can and will create that reality. Now more than ever we need faith that this is so. I know this is so."

That is what I do now. With our ring in my hand I pray for strength and I pray for mercy and I envisage a village free from demise, where once again we live in the bliss of normality. Grant my wish God. May my faith be constant.

God bless: Matthew Hands, Elizabeth Thorpe, Margaret Bands, Mary Thorpe, Syth Torre, William Thorpe, Richard Sydall, William Torre, Annie Torre, John Sydall, Ellen Sydall, Humphrey Hawkesworth, Martha Bands, Jonathan Ragge, Humphrey Torre, Thomas Thorpe, Mary Bands, Elizabeth Sydall, Alice Ragge, Alice Sydall.

1st November 1665

October turns to November and a bitter chill has set in. There is talk that the cold weather will make perish this pestilence that has itself made perish so many amongst us. The total buried now is twenty-nine but still the Stubbs and Rowlands are at present waging battle against the disease. So many families are now, like our own, dismembered; some are annihilated completely as this evil sickness sweeps from household to household, paying no heed to either age or position.

Mother continues to visit the sick and grieving, though she returns earlier now and spends some hours before supper with Joseph and myself. Catherine or Rowland are often in attendance, being frequent visitors both. They gently encourage her to engage in conversation on matters that might be of interest to her but that do not bring to mind the loss she has suffered, though I am sure they are ever present in her thoughts as they are in mine. The days and weeks pass in a melancholy that weighs heavy.

There is the mask of relief in sleep, a forgetfulness. Oft times I dream that all is as it once was. It is summer once more and we are all at the delf. The children are paddling in the streams, nets in hand, happy and careless. There are Sarah and Ellen, helping the younger ones to cross on stepping-stones. Alice holds tightly to Sarah's hand, anxious and concentrated, whilst Richard bounds on fearlessly. Elizabeth sits upon the bank overlooking the scene with amusement, shouting out the occasional instruction. Catherine and I read a book together upon the picnic blanket. I feel blissful. I feel the sun and the wind upon me. I hear the laughter and cries of the children. I am light as the air. I am happy. And for a fleeting moment when I awake I am happy still... Then I remember. The happiness drains from me. Misery and heaviness return. My bleeding heart is broken all over again.

12th November 1665

We are nigh midpoint through November and only three more are passed: Hugh Stubbs on the first, Alice Teylour on the third and Hannah Rowland on the fifth day of this month. Seeds of hope are planted and people go about their business with heads held a little higher.

The cold is severe and I think often of those poor souls who are camped in the fields and hillsides, too fearful to return. Some families that sought shelter further afield with friends or relatives, have found on arrival that they are unwelcome and have been forced to return forthwith. They have been shunned rather by the rest of the villagers for their desertion, but I am sure it is a false morality, for many would have done the very same if they thought there was the slightest chance of their being safely harboured until the present threat were dissipated.

Catherine and I spent the morning making a new batch of plague water and poultices. We follow recipes sent from relatives of her husband in London. The poultice is prepared by hollowing out an onion into which a fig is placed it is then wrapped in wet paper. Before applying it to the tumour, it is to be heated in embers and applied hot. Three or four of these should be applied consecutively and left upon the sore for three to four hours. Supposedly it is effective in drawing the poison to the centre so that it might ripen and break; and being broke, the infection will come away. The plague water is a more complicated affair and needs to be left for just over a week and then distilled before it can be taken. We steep flowers, seeds and roots with a peck of green walnuts in wine. When ready it is poured into glass vials to be distributed.

Whilst preparing the poultice, Catherine informed me that the latest villager to leave and make shelter in the fields is Andrew Merrill. He, being entirely without dependants, has constructed a sort of shed from unwanted materials, gathered it seems over the last month or so, from friends and neighbours. He has set up home upon the sloping common land behind the church, right next to the far hedge so as to benefit from its natural sheltering of the wind and rain. He has elected to spend the long winter months cold and alone with apparently only his cockerel for company. At least here I have Mother, Catherine and Rowland to converse with, the warmth of the hearth and the shelter of my home, all be it greatly changed and seeming rather unfamiliar.

26th November 1665

I have taken to long afternoon walks accompanied at times by Catherine. The mornings I spend at chores in the rectory whilst Catherine, armed with a basket full of poultices, plague water and oatcakes, accompanies her husband in his rounds of comforting the afflicted and grieving. After lunch Mr. Mompesson continues his duties, usually in the company of the former rector Rev. Thomas Stanley. Reverend Stanley, following the death of his wife, had not long moved back to the village before it was struck down with plague. Catherine usually spends time with George and Elizabeth but on occasions, when the housemaid is not occupied, she accompanies Joseph and I up onto the hills.

I strap Joseph to my back in the manner I oft witnessed used by the field workers at harvest time. Using an old tablecloth discarded by the late Mrs. Stanley and recovered by Catherine from the attic, I forge a harness which he sits in, legs astride. Secured thus by a tight knot around my midriff I find I can walk quite considerable distances unperturbed.

As we made our way through the village I could not help but notice how changed it appears.

The tracks where carriages and carts once ran are now started to become overgrown by weed and grass. All manner of livestock may be encountered roaming the streets: chickens, cows, goats and sheep, all unkempt and uncared for. There is a strange quiet to the place. No sounds of children inventing imaginary games with sticks or stones. All traders in unnecessary commodities have put down tools, some shops are left abandoned. Houses that have been, or are presently visited, have white crosses smeared upon their doors. They stand shut up with curtains drawn and no snakes of smoke are to be seen trailing upwards from their chimneys as is habitual at this time of year. Buildings that were undergoing repair or improvement stand idle, as if time itself had suddenly stopped. Gardens are untended. Fruit decomposes on the branches and vegetables rot in the ground. Some of the beehives now lying dormant have been partly dismantled for firewood. There is no preparation for the future, no planning for that which might not be.

It is only when we have put some distance between ourselves and our pitiful community that we allow ourselves to breathe deeply, to take in big lungfuls of fresh, clean, uninfected air. It is wonderful upon those hills; the sky is bright and endless and from my feet to the horizon stretches the promise of another world. For those few hours a sort of calm descends upon us all. I looked today down on Stoney Middleton and imagined Rowland there, employed in his father's mill. I saw a time when he would hang up his apron, bid farewell to his colleagues and cheerfully start his journey home. To our home where I would be waiting for him and as I did so, I whispered onto the breeze, "Wait for me Rowland. Wait for me." Dear Lord may this be Your will and may Your will be done.

It is always with some dread that I turn and head back to the village, back to our cruel reality.

The winter sun was setting as we began our descent, we stopped to bear witness. An enormous globe, slowly sinking behind a row of trees silhouetted on the skyline, their branches intertwined; an orange ball of light, whose warm glow was perceivable only through that tree-woven veil of black lace, overhanging Eyam. As I watched, suddenly my heart lifted to recognise, to be reminded of beauty once more. If only I could have stayed in that moment, in that 'now'. The pains of the past erased, the threats of the future forgotten. I felt then something akin to peace. My soul yearns for peace.

14th November 1665

It will not be easy to find comfort in sleep this night for an image most frightful is etched in my mind's eye. Despite all the horror I have hitherto witnessed, it seems that I am not yet immune.

On my return from the rectory this afternoon I heard the distressed cries and delirious screams of some poor soul in the last throes of pestilence. Though this in itself was nothing to remark upon, it being an all too common sound in these times, I was confused for it seemed not to be emitting from a particular location but rather approaching me at some speed from behind.

As the wailing grew louder I was proven not to be mistaken and so gave an about turn to determine the fact. So startled was I by what I saw that I could neither move nor avert my eyes. Running down the street, with not a stitch of clothing about his person, was the emaciated frame of an elderly man. Frozen to the spot as I was, I failed to take any evasive action and before I knew it this pitiful figure, this awful apparition, was upon me. The flesh that hung from his bones bore blemishes and upon his chest I noticed the token, the stamp of death. His face had the look of a madman and his enormous eyes rolled uncontrollably in their sunken sockets, his shoulder-length hair was matted with a foul smelling substance and spittle ran from the corners of his mouth. He seemed to know neither which way to turn nor what to do. His arms flung wildly about him and though he appeared at times to look directly at me, it seemed he saw me not.

A ghastly vision it was, such that might have come straight from some awful nightmare. I felt my skin turn clammy and my heart beat so, that I was afeared it might burst in my chest. I had just recovered my wits and was about to take flight when a second figure appeared behind the wretched being and began to steer him back in the direction from whence he came. The woman, who I now saw to be Mrs. Stubbs, gave me an apologetic look as she led him away and it was then that I recognised her fellow creature to be John Stubbs, her husband. So ravaged was he by this most dreadful of maladies, in both body and mind, that I had failed to identify the distorted features before me.

I feel yet a little shaken and the image in my mind's eye haunts me still.

29th November 1665

It having turned so bitterly cold, the ground is now quite frozen and I hear that the digging of the graves for our dead has become a nigh impossible task. The sexton has called upon all men fit and well to assist in the digging. It has been rumoured that the graves of those who have other family members that are too stricken, are covered only lightly in soil so that the same grave may, if necessary, be used more than once.

Many of the men have heeded the call for help and taken up their shovels. Mr. Howe is said to do the work of three men. Mr. Daniel has also been aiding in the task. Mother and I passed him on his way home this afternoon, spade in hand, looking quite exhausted and downcast. He described it as being a 'sorry task' to have to be digging the tombs of your friends and neighbours and expressed his ruefulness at the fact that their funerals were but brief affairs, quite lacking in the ceremony they deserved. Mother tried to rally him by telling him that it was a fine act to be aiding the sexton in his job and that the families were no doubt mightily grateful to him, for what otherwise would become of the corpses of their loved ones if men such as he were disinclined to undertake such a business? Mr. Daniel merely nodded in recognition, and with limbs so heavy as to be made of lead, slowly continued his homeward journey. What a forlorn sight his slight figure made as it plodded cumbersomely up the hill, the spade balanced upon his left shoulder being almost as big as he.

"Poor man," exclaimed Mother. "He has seen enough of graves, his first-born dying in infancy and the second at birth, his wife with it."

"As have we all," I replied, the words escaping from my lips before I had chance to heed them. We continued our journey home, both in silent reflection.

God bless: Hugh Stubbs, Alice Teylour, Hannah Rowland, John Stubbs, Anne Stubbs Elizabeth Warrington, Randoll Danyell.

4th December 1665

We awoke this morning to discover a thick layer of snow lying upon the ground. Although not the first this winter, it is definitely the deepest. This afternoon, Rowland and I decided to wrap up and climb up to Riley woods. I put layers of clothes upon Joseph and with him strapped to me, we set off. How white and unspoilt was the snow with barely a footprint to break its spread. It glistened and sparkled in the afternoon sun; a robe fit for a princess clothed the countryside.

On our ascent we encountered the Reverend Stanley. Although no longer the reverend appointed to our parish, everyone still holds him in particularly high regard and he is very much respected by all, him being of a very fair and most upright character. He stopped to offer his condolences for our loss and to enquire as to the health of my mother. As he did so I could not help but notice how his eyes were fixed to the corner of material that formed the harness I had made for Joseph. I glanced down to see what might be distracting him so. There, embroidered in blue stitching, were the initials A.S. He had obviously recognised these as those of his dearly beloved, and now deceased wife, Anne. At once I felt the heat of guilt sweep over me as if caught red-handed at the scene of some crime. For a minute I knew not quite what to say, so awkward and flustered was I at having been discovered. When I had recovered a little I explicated, in sentences stilted by my embarrassment, how Catherine and I had come to discover the tablecloth, discarded and forgotten, in the attic of the rectory. After what seemed an interminable time of stuttering and stumbling over my explanation, Mr. Stanley smiled kindly and pronounced:

"Dear Miss Sydall, please do not fret so for it is quite the best use I have ever seen made of what I consider to be, such a superfluous object. Indeed, I have never understood why a table, on which is spilt crumbs and oft tarnished with mead or ale, one would want to lay a cloth, which cannot be wiped down with a rag, but needs rather to be freshly laundered after nearly every sitting. My dear wife, I am sure, was of quite the same persuasion and hence I suppose proceeded to bury it in the attic amidst other such futile possessions. I am glad to see it put to such a good at last!"

How relieved I was to hear those well-meant words that secured my acquittal and offered me the peace of mind afforded only to the forgiven. We commented briefly upon the freshness of the day and the beauty of the snow and then continued upon our paths. Rowland was quite amused by the whole exchange and teased me cruelly for what he considered to be my exaggerated guilt.

"It's but a tablecloth Emmott, not the crown jewels!" He laughed.

Upon reaching Riley woods, Rowland and I gathered sprigs of holly. We laid them in a pile in a small clearing. Just as we were about to leave, Rowland spied a clump of mistletoe sheltering high in the branches of a beech tree. Being much used to scaling trees as a child he made light work of the climb. The descent however was not so easy, it being done backwards with a large bunch of mistletoe clenched between his teeth. I shouted guidance from the safety of the forest floor and eventually he was once again with feet on solid ground. He, for his efforts, held the mistletoe above my head and was duly rewarded with a kiss.

I have stored the mistletoe and holly in the outhouse so that it might be a surprise for Mother. I will decorate the house with it a few days before Christmas. No doubt it will be a quieter and sadder affair for all of us this year.

12th December 1665

Whilst at chores in the rectory this morning a frantic ringing and knocking was heard at the parlour door. Indeed, Bridget the housemaid had barely pulled it ajar when young Mr. Rowe hurtled into the room. The poor man was in a terrible state and could barely make himself understood such was his panic. After a short time we managed to ascertain that his wife Mary had gone into labour that morning and through fear of infection, no midwife would assist.

"I am no midwife, Mr. Rowe," asserted Catherine, "but I have borne two infants of my own. Emmott, fetch some clean cloth from the cupboard."

I quickly followed her instruction and the three of us flew through the door and down the road to the small cottage that was their home. Mrs. Rowe looked to be in the final stages of her labour. Having witnessed and aided three of Mother's births, I too was no stranger to the process. Fortunately, the panting and howling does not affect us women folk in the same way as it does the men, who it seems are so terrified by the sounds of childbirth that they are rendered quite helpless by it. Mr. Rowe stood beside us flapping and pacing for a while, then, upon being reassured that there was nothing untoward in his wife's behaviour, he promptly left the room.

Catherine immediately set to work in lifting and parting the woman's legs. I laid the clean cloth beneath her for we could already see the babe's head. Catherine and I gave words of encouragement as poor Mary was in much pain and verily frightened, it being her first child. I judged from the state of the sheets, which were drenched in perspiration and the fact that she seemed much weakened and tired, that she had been in labour for some time. Catherine and I exchanged anxious glances.

"Mary, you must push, do you hear me? The next time you feel the pain you must purse your lips and push with all your strength. Do not waste your energy on cries; you must push your babe out."

Catherine's stern but softly spoken words seemed to work, for on the next contraction the babe's head was born, and two more heaves accompanied by stifled screams saw the infant safely delivered. Mother, though exhausted, was both relieved and delighted at hearing the baby's first cries, as indeed were Catherine and myself. After wiping him down (for indeed it was a boy that was delivered), I swaddled the newly born in the remaining piece of clean cloth and then carefully handed him to his mother. I then informed the young Mr. Rowe of the good news and requested him to find a sharp knife and to hold the blade of it to a flame for a good few minutes, so that it might be used to cut the cord; this act I completed myself, having witnessed it being used on more than one occasion to separate my younger siblings from our mother. After the tether was cleanly broken, Catherine delivered the afterbirth. I never cease to wonder at the size of this enormous liver-like lump of flesh which slithered onto the sheet and was hastily collected and deposited into the chamber pot which lay beside the bed. Catherine then left to scrub her hands which were covered in fresh blood. On her return I took leave and descended the stairs to wash myself. Mr. Rowe was just entering with a clean bucket of water and hard brush, to this he added some warm water that had been heating upon the hearth. I scrubbed my hands and lower arms until they were nigh raw and then made my way back upstairs followed by Mr. Rowe, who was by now keen to see his son.

As we entered the gloomy room, Mary had the child to her breast. I approached the bed to steal a better look at the small child that had just been bought into this world. It was then that I noted the purplish blotch upon Mary's chest. I unwittingly took a sharp intake of breath upon which Catherine grabbed and squeezed my arm, keeping her gaze all the while on the suckling infant. William Rowe smiled down proudly on the scene, oblivious it would seem to the token that marked their fate. Mary watched in wonder as her newborn son partook of his first meal. Catherine and I congratulated the couple and made our exit, promising to call again shortly. We walked in silence back to the rectory, shocked and deeply saddened.

Back in the kitchen Catherine insisted that we undress before the hearth and launder the clothes we had been wearing. She asked Bridget to fetch some fresh clothes for the two of us. Whilst in a state of undress, we filled a tub with warm water and set to scrubbing at our skin with soaked flannel. We scrubbed hard, not with frenzy through fear but rather through anger, anger at the injustice of a world that can be so cruel.

I wonder now how they fare. In my hand I hold our ring and I pray for them; I pray also to God to keep strong my faith.

14th December 1665

As we had arranged yesterday, Catherine and I met early at the church gates in order to pay a visit upon the Rowe's. On our arrival we found the door to be open and so walked straight into the kitchen, calling out our greetings as we did so. We were immediately silenced however by the scene of the young Mr. Rowe, sat head in hands, at the table. He lifted his head and as his glance met ours, he simply shook his head. His face and indeed his whole miserable countenance affirmed our worst fears.

Nervously we mounted the stairs and upon entering the bedroom we found Mary half delirious with grief or fever, or perhaps both, the tiny infant clasped to her breast, its face was waxen and its limbs hung loose in final repose. Catherine tried to prise the babe from its mother's arms but she held it in a vice like clasp and merely became more agitated and began blaspheming before Catherine. Luckily, Catherine was wise enough to not take offence at the afflicted woman's curses and instead stroked her head maternally and convinced her with gentle words that her baby needed to be put down, so as they both might benefit from some rest. Eventually she became calmer and with some reluctance still, handed over her baby to Catherine who immediately passed it to me so she might then concern herself with settling Mary into her bed. Once done, still mumbling almost inaudibly, she drifted into a fevered sleep. The babe was limp, cold and lifeless in my arms and called to my mind Elizabeth's toy doll that she and Alice had been playing with in front of the hearth only a month or so before. It is a queer thing to see how after death from this most dreadful of diseases, the corpse does not stiffen as is normally the case. Even after passing it proves to be the most unnatural of afflictions that I have hereto witnessed.

Downstairs once more we advised Mr. Rowe that the babe should be buried this very day and Catherine assured him that she would make arrangements with her husband for it to be interred that same afternoon. William Rowe did not look at the infant but nodded in agreement and then informed us that Mr. Mompesson should go ahead with the burial, but he would remain here with his wife. With that, Catherine placed a hand upon his arm and we left with the babe still in my arms. We decided to take it directly to the church and lay it out in the vestry as Catherine did not want her children to be witness to such a tragedy.

This evening as Mother and I prepared the potage for supper we heard the passing bell toll. We fell silent a while to pay our respects to that tiny baby boy who had not even a name given to him.

16th December 1665

I took Joseph to the rectory with me this morning. The snow at last has cleared from the hillsides but in the village it leaves a dirty, muddy slush. Bridget opened the door to us as Mr. Mompesson was already gone to pay a visit to the young Mr. and Mrs. Rowe, and Catherine was occupied with a new batch of plague water. We found her busy in the kitchen, the table laid out with jars. I placed Joseph on the rug which lay in front of the hearth and gave him a few wooden spoons and other utensils with which to amuse himself. Catherine and I then spent a good part of the morning distilling and decanting the remedy. We had just finished and were about placing the jars on a shelf, made empty for the purpose in the larder, when Mr. Mompesson appeared in the doorway.

He wore a grave look on his face and as we turned to him he informed us of the demise of Mary that night, and of her husband who has taken to their bed and cannot be induced to rise.

"I cannot persuade him to take neither liquid nor solid, he seems determined to lay there until he is reunited with his family in God's care."

Upon the utterance of these words he turned dejectedly and retired to his study where he spent the rest of the morning. Catherine informed me that he would spend the next coming hours in silent contemplation and reflection, a daily habit that he has practised, she related, for many years, he insisting that it makes clear his soul's intention, binding him ever closer to God.

Catherine tells me that Mr. Mompesson keeps a record book in his study of all deaths. Even with the chime of the church bell or the short funeral procession that passes by our window, it is true that many of us have lost count of our death toll, so frequent are the occurrences. Death has become most commonplace. It has lost its veil of mystery and has been somewhat unarmed, for though we feel sorrow and grief on the loss of our loved ones, there is no longer a display of shock or disbelief. The dissolution of those we know but hold not so dear in our hearts, is, upon being communicated, accepted all too easily and excites scarcely any notice for we are hardened by its continuous repetition. Like the vials we fill that would eventually flow over, it seems there is only so much grief we can hold in our hearts.

22nd December 1665

On arrival at the vicarage yesterday morning Catherine informed me that after a brief and very half- hearted struggle poor William Rowe was now reunited with his dear family. I took some solace in the knowledge that his grief was short borne.

This morning Catherine and I decorated the rectory with the help of George and Elizabeth who were very much excited by the festive preparations. The parlour has branches of holly and tendrils of ivy hanging from the cross beams and they have even a small branch of yew, acquired from the common woodland, that stands proudly in the corner. Elizabeth and George fashioned snowflakes and stars from some discarded cloth and parchment and have hung them from the branches; how pretty the room now looks and how wonderful to hear the excited exclamations of the children so happily preoccupied. My heart was at the same time lightened by their enchantment yet made also heavy by the memories of such activities and merriment that once filled our own home.

This afternoon, whilst Mother was out making gift of some freshly baked bread to those too distracted by grief or too busy nursing their sick to have time or inclination to produce their own, Rowland and I laid and hung the holly and mistletoe that we had gathered from Riley woods some weeks before. It did make the house look more cheerful, though I was rather nervous of Mother's reaction upon her return. Maybe this year she would rather pretend that the festive season was not upon us, or even worse, that she might think it distasteful and vulgar to adorn the rooms that were once so full of life.

It was just before supper that Mother entered the parlour. She removed her outer coat and hung it upon its usual peg by the door. Rowland and I stood fixated and unsure by the far wall, awaiting her response. As she turned and took in the scene, her features hardened slightly. I held my breath. For an instant I wished we had not been so foolish as to think that our indulgence would please Mother, however, before the thought had time to take root in my mind, I perceived the broad smile that crept slowly across her face.

"Oh Emmott, Rowland, thank you, that looks very fine!"

Those being her exact words. Relieved and gladdened, we all partook heartily of supper this evening.

25th December 1665

Mother, Joseph and I attended Christmas mass this morning. The church was packed, all who could attend being, I believe, present. Catherine had decorated the interior with garlands of ivy and holly. It was a dark, dreary and bitterly cold morning, though the numerous candles dotted about in every possible corner and crevice, threw a warm, orange glow around the place. For some reason it called to my mind the story of Jonah in the belly of the whale. In the pulpit stood the Reverend Mompesson and at the foot of the steps to his left stood the Reverend Stanley.

Catherine informs me that Mr. Mompesson and his incumbent spend more and more time together in their visits to the sick and grieving and indeed, stay up late into the night discussing and debating their faith. She says that though they are poles apart in their religious outlooks (Mr. Stanley being known for his fervently held and more orthodox views, standing in stark contrast to the more liberal and unorthodox standpoint taken by her husband), they have great respect for one another. Both men have come to recognise that it is not the details of texts and ways of worship that are important but rather the acting on the fundamental message of love, compassion and humanity. They have come to the agreement it seems, that the key message of the Bible is found in the statement 'Do unto others as you would have them do unto you'. As a moral yardstick it has, they conclude, no superior and they have used it continually to aid in their decision making in these unprecedented times. How simple it is yet how difficult to apply, being intrinsically selfish as we are.

Mr. Mompesson's voice seemed to rebound off the stone walls and echo through the damp air. His service did not part from tradition but was delivered in a most heartfelt fashion that failed not to move every member of the congregation. Mr. Stanley read psalm one hundred and twenty one from the Good Book and after we sang a Christmas hymn. Each and every one of us stood tall and sang aloud with pride and strength, so that God himself might hear us and take pity enough to end our terrible plight.

Near the end of the service the Reverend Mompesson read aloud the names of all those hereto deceased. As he did so, the face of each individual passed before my eyes, the young, the old and amongst them, of course, our own dear loved ones. I do believe by the end there was not a dry eye to be had in the place. The men sniffed and stared, eyes downcast and the women dabbed at theirs with their kerchiefs. The service ended with a prayer, a prayer for the souls of all those departed, for strength and perseverance to face whatever might follow and a plea that, on this day when we celebrate His son entering our world, God in his benevolence might see fit to release us from this pestilence. The final Amen was a subdued whisper; as I uttered mine, I squeezed my hands tightly together in supplication.

Mother stopped awhile to converse with Mr. Daniel who happened to pass through the arched doorway at the same time as we made our exit. It being so cold a morning I bundled Joseph in my arms and hastened homewards. Rowland would be calling later and I wanted to prepare myself and the house for his visit. The thought that I would see him soon cheered me greatly and warmed my entire being which had been otherwise so chilled this Christmas morning.

It seems like ourselves, that the Yuletide celebrations were at large kept within the confines of people's houses this year. Unnecessary public gatherings being now mostly avoided, they being suspected to speed the spread of infection, and few in any case having the heart for them. Some of the men folk I am told supped a while together at their preferred tavern but most stayed at home in front of the fire, the wind being particularly biting.

Rowland came to spend the evening with us and bought with him the fowl that he had promised which we roasted over the fire. Before supper, Mother too offered a prayer for those loved ones no longer with us. We remembered the Rowes and the Blackwells, whose youngest was taken from them only last evening, a family that up until then had remained untouched by the pestilence. Poor Anthony Blackwell must have succumbed rapidly for Elizabeth, who had been such a good friend to our own dear departed, had called only two days prior to enquire after our well-being and to offer us a gift of a small jar of honey, collected from their hives last summer. On enquiring after her family she assured us they were all in good health.

After having feasted we sat around the hearth and spread some of the honey that Elizabeth had kindly given onto chunks of bread. How sweet it tasted. The more so for bringing to mind memories of that most pleasant summer past, when all was so different from the dark sufferings we now endure. Little Joseph enjoyed his greatly and we laughed as he left honey finger marks all over the kitchen until he managed to lick them all completely clean.

Rowland left quite soon after supper. I would have had him leave much earlier for by then it had begun to snow quite heavily. He had, however, insisted on staying until the festivities had terminated and assured me he had tread the path so often that he would be able to find his way home blindfolded. Fortunately, his boast was not tested for with the full moon reflecting upon the freshly laid snow, he must have been able to see his way through the village and across the fields quite clearly.

Minutes after I had shut the door on Rowland there was a knocking upon it. Thinking that Rowland had mislaid or forgotten some item I opened the door, fully expecting to see him stood there before me. I was therefore surprised to find instead Mr. Daniel at the threshold and armed with what looked like a small bottle of mead. On seeing my surprise, he very sheepishly wished me good tidings and enquired as to whether Elizabeth, he then corrected himself, my mother, might be at home. Quite where else he thought she might be at this hour I cannot tell. On turning to call her, I jumped to find her standing directly behind me, her face considerably brightened and at once quite youthful in complexion. Over my head I could not help but remark how warmly they smiled into each other's eyes.

It being by this time quite late, I made my excuses and settled firstly Joseph and then myself to bed. As I write this I can faintly hear their whispered exchanges and my heart is warmed to hear on occaision Mother's soft laughter rise from the kitchen and permeate these emptied rooms once again. On this, the Lord's birthday, I pray that we might be reborn into happier times.

God bless: John Rowbotham, Baby Rowe, Mary Rowe, William Rowe, Thomas Wilson, William Rowbotham, Anthony Blackwell.

2nd January 1666

On my walk to the rectory I find the latest house to be standing empty is the Rowbotham's. The father and three sons have all now perished, two of the sons Robert and Daniel having passed on the first day of this New Year. Their mother, it is said, has taken to living with relatives in one of the pest houses up on the common land. The bitter cold it seems has only fought to slow the disease in its dreaded course around the village, rather than to have annihilated it altogether as we all had hoped.

Catherine has received news once more from Mr. Mompesson's uncle in Sheffield who is again urging her and the children to take refuge with his family. She has at last conceded to her husband's wishes, in part at least, as she remains adamant that she will not abandon her husband and friends in the village, though he is desperate to see her too harboured at a safe distance. She is shrewd for she has persuaded her husband that it is God's will that she stay at his side and help the village in its time of need. This she has made her purpose in life, as she explained to me with a passion I have n'er seen from her until today but which failed to surprise me, for I have learnt that Catherine is, like a rose flower, comprised of many layers.

"How I have prayed to God for years Emmott, that I might be of service to others, for this is my want and my joy. I will not and cannot renounce it now for of this horror inflicted upon us, I might make some good and realise my true purpose."

She knows that her husband might argue against her until there is no breath left in his body but he cannot argue against the very God he has sworn to serve.

She confided today that they are looking at arrangements into sending the children away along with their housemaid Bridget. Apparently, the reverend Stanley has arranged for a carriage that is making journey to Sheffield a week on Tuesday to take them. Poor Catherine, she will surely miss them so terribly, but to know they are safe would also bring her such peace of mind for naturally she worries for them dreadfully.

Perhaps it is the new year that is making us more resolute but I too have come to a decision and have determined to bid Rowland to visit no more. Though it is harsh, I am intent on my decision. I am in need of a promise to pull me forwards; something to hold on to like a floating twig might offer refuge to a fallen leaf upon a swollen brook. I am in need of a future, a future for the two of us. If that were taken from me I cannot imagine how I might overcome such a loss, after all that is already lost to me. I can no longer have him risk his life in coming to visit.

Catherine and I discussed the matter in great detail and we have both made the decision to protect those we love as best we can. I have resolved to tell Rowland on the morrow.

5th January 1666

Poor Rowland, as soon as we met today he could tell something was amiss. At first he feared that myself, Joseph or Mother were taken ill and his relief was apparent when I assured him that it was not the case. On explaining the cause for my apparent loss of colour and thumping heartbeat, that he felt immediately as he held me to him, his expression once again turned to one of confusion and concern.

It took me nigh on an hour to persuade him of my earnestness and the matter was only resolved after I gave my solemn promise that I would meet him up on the hillside at the village boundary every other day upon his lunch hour. To be sure that the miasma would not contaminate him, I told him that he must wait at the sycamore tree with the fallen branch and I at the village gate by the boundary stone, so that from my very breath he might be safe. We agreed on a sign which was that I would hold up three fingers if we were all still well, two if Mother or Joseph took ill and one if heaven forbid, they were both afflicted. The day I appear as arranged, wearing his ring, will, we agreed, be a sign that at last this dreadful evil scourge which has so blighted us has taken leave and our new life is ready to begin. Oh that this day comes soon.

We held each other close all afternoon and on his departure that evening I verily believe he took with him my heart. In its place lays an empty, deflated sack that against all logic weighs twice as heavy. As I watched him walk away he shouted confidently over his shoulder.

"Mark my words Emmott, next Wakes' tide you will be my wife."

Dear God that his words be proven to be true. Each night I kiss our ring and then carefully wrap it back in its handkerchief, waiting for the time when I might place it upon my finger and leave it there forever more.

12th January 1666

Catherine is very subdued these past days. It seems that the relief she feels in knowing her children to be safely arrived and installed with Mr. Bielby and his kin in Sheffield cannot outweigh the ache in her heart at their separation. Never before have I witnessed her to be so lacking in spirit, it is most unlike her. She continues her visits and nursing of the sick but her countenance is quite altered.

This afternoon I helped her to tidy and stack the children's belongings in the nursery. How large and empty the room seemed as we collected them up and organised them into neat piles. How poignant to see Elizabeth's much loved doll lying prostrate upon the floor and George's wooden soldier on its back, eyes staring blankly at the ceiling. Amongst the abandoned toys, Catherine came across Elizabeth's favourite story book. Upon opening the cover we discovered the words 'Eliza book' scrawled in childish hand. Catherine's eyes immediately filled with tears and as she clutched it to her breast I put an arm around her. We sat upon the wooden toy box and she calmly relayed to me how she had observed their departure from an upstairs window. She watched them as they mounted the carriage with Bridget and were encouraged to settle to their seats, a confused look upon their faces. From her vantage point she saw the door slammed shut, the horses set to and the carriage slowly draw away until it disappeared around the bend and out of sight. At this point she told of how suddenly she became overwhelmed with the conviction that she would never again in this lifetime set eyes upon her dear children.

In all honesty I knew not how best to console her for it would be foolish to offer any kind of promise given our situation. She sniffed violently and wiped her eyes, then looking straight into mine she said,

"How self indulgent of me Emmott that I should shed tears for loved ones who are now safe, when so many are shedding tears for loved ones forever lost."

Upon these words she regained composure and set herself once again to task. I begin to lose count of how many times I have witnessed this desolate scene, of people brushing themselves off, rubbing themselves down and propelling themselves forwards, when in fact what they really want to do is crumple into a collapsed heap and abandon themselves to their grief. As I put George's broken boat into its box I wondered how many times we could have the wind taken from our sails, only then to set forth once again upon our destined route, before once again we are left to drift and finally succumb to be wrecked upon some unknown shore. All hope lost and past caring.

16th January 1666

Catherine seems much recovered and is quite herself again. I have remarked of late, when at the rectory, that in the undertaking of their daily business both she and Mr. Mompesson have a newly acquired air of purpose and resoluteness about their demeanour.

As we took one of our walks about the delf this afternoon, Catherine confided that her husband, in conjunction with his incumbent, Mr. Thomas Stanley, have these past days been deep in discourse on how best we might organise ourselves in dealing with this dreadful state of affairs that afflicts our village. They have apparently been in correspondence with the Earl of Devonshire at Chatsworth House and are shortly to call the whole village to a meeting, in order to propose a course of action. Catherine is unsure as to the details of their plan but has been assured by her husband that the Earl has pledged his allegiance to the cause and given word that he will assist in whatever means are deemed necessary. Indeed, she seems somewhat revived by the whole course of events. I cannot help but wonder what their plan of action might be but am convinced it will be for the best of all concerned and they will be heeded to, the both, though as chalk and cheese, being deemed most upright in character and sound of judgement.

Upon our return to the village we encountered Mr. Merrill and his feathered companion. The cockerel, at least, looked in fine health though Mr. Merrill it seemed was not faring the harsh winter quite so well in his makeshift home upon the hillside. He is all skin and bone and in need of a thorough wash, his clothing is reduced to mere rags and his hair completely matted and having hedge debris entangled within its tresses. All of these factors culminated to produce a rather alarming vision, being so feral as he was in appearance. On noticing our presence, he nodded swiftly and hurriedly scampered inside, back to the sanctuary of his hovel abode. Whether this was through shame of his appearance or from fear of contagion I am not quite sure. Perhaps it were a mix of the both.

I have told Catherine of the arrangement to which Rowland and I have agreed. Upon divulging the details she insisted that on our days of meeting I am to leave my chores at the rectory earlier, so I might return home at the normal hour and not arouse suspicion in Mother. Dear Catherine, a truer friend could not be found, so understanding is she of my motives and how absolute in her support of my actions.

Mother seems a little stronger and is not so often to be found sat, staring blankly at the wall. She visits the sick or bereaved in the morning and after lunch is more oft than not to be found at the communal oven, making bread or oatcakes to take with her on the morrow. Most evenings we prepare supper together and she begins to converse more freely and less distractedly, the air of solemnity that seemed to envelope her whole being appears to be slowly lifting.

Mr. Daniel calls quite frequently and has recently begun to take it upon himself to make any repairs needed about the home. Last week he replaced the latch upon my bedroom window which had broken clean off, thus making it impossible to fully close so that an icy draught persisted. At present he is upon the roof of the outhouse, fixing a leak. Oft times he brings with him supplies of wood or coal that he stacks neatly in a corner of the outhouse. A month or so ago I was anxious that we had not enough logs and fuel in reserve to see us through 'til spring, the weather as it is, being most severe. Thanks to Mr. Daniel we have not yet been without heat one evening this winter and our stock will now last the cold season and longer if needed.

Mother invites Mr. Daniel to take supper with us. He living alone has only himself to feed and from his slight build it would suggest that oft times he tends not to bother. He is always seen off with a loaf of bread and freshly baked batch of cakes or biscuits carefully wrapped in muslin. He is a shy man who is sparing with his words. At the table he reddens slightly if addressed directly and retorts in clipped sentences uttered under his breath, so rendering himself almost inaudible and making it hard to comprehend that which has been said. When he is invited, I retire early taking Joseph with me and leave him and Mother to stack and clean. It is customary now that he stays a while and shares a hot drink with Mother by the hearth. Always on these occasions, as on that first night at Christmas, I hear intermittently Mother's soft laughter breaking through over the low murmurings of conversation and I am truly gladdened by it.

19th January 1666

Edythe and Edward Taylor's baby was born in the early hours of yesterday morning. Mother happened upon Widow Cooper this morning who proudly informed her of the new arrival, a baby girl who is to be named Sarah Ann. Mother related that Widow Cooper had aided Edythe's mother in the delivery of the infant, she being awakened by a frenzied knocking upon her door nigh on midnight. On arriving at Edythe's bedside it was clear to her that she was nearing the final stage of her labour and an hour or so later, following only a handful of pushes, the child was successfully delivered into this world.

By the time they had cleared up and Widow Cooper was leaving, both mother and baby were sleeping peacefully. Apparently the child took to the breast directly and once so sated fell peacefully into slumber. Mrs. Taylor was busying herself in the preparation of a potage so that Edythe might regain her strength as quickly as possible. Edward, it was told, is delighted at the arrival of his daughter, claiming in her a strong resemblance to himself. Widow Cooper tells that the child was born with a healthy mop of dark hair and it being widely understood that a newborn bares the likeness of its father directly after birth, she is certain that the small mite will eventually take on the features of her mother. Either way, Widow Cooper declares that she has not seen a babe born equal in pleasantness of appearance. They usually being, in her opinion, more akin to 'a rat plucked by its tail from a pitcher of water!'

Catherine and I hope to pay visit to the newborn on the morrow or overmorrow, though Widow Cooper has informed us that Edythe is not keen on receiving visitors, so scared is she that they may infect the babe.

This afternoon I climbed up to the village boundary to see Rowland. I shouted to him at the top of my voice, "Edythe and Edward Taylor." Simultaneously I mimed the rocking of a babe in arms. Sometimes if the wind be blowing in the right direction, our voices might be carried upon it and reach the ears of the other. Today it blew from behind me and surely Rowland caught my meaning for he raised both hands above his head and applauded. He surely had a smile upon his face also, but from such a distance I was unable to discern it. We lingered not long today. The gusts of air slapped and stung my cheeks with their icy-cold hands as I turned in haste to make my descent.

21st January 1666

Catherine and I paid visit to Edythe and Edward this afternoon to welcome their new arrival. On entering the house, Edward proclaimed that both mother and daughter were doing well. As we made our way to the foot of the stairs Edward began to look uneasy. He thence announced that Edythe was not keen on receiving visitors so scared was she that her firstborn might become infected with the distemper.

"She is insistent that all remain behind the threshold to the chamber where they are laid, I hope this does no offence to the both of you," he uttered awkwardly.

On assuring him that we understood and that indeed no offence was taken, we proceeded to mount the stairs. The bedroom door lay ajar and upon knocking and announcing our arrival we slowly pushed it to. Edythe beamed at us from beneath the bed cover and held her precious bundle aloft. From our vantage point in the hallway we could easily discern the small, puckered face, wigged it seemed by an abundant mop of black hair. Indeed the infant was verily a picture of health and loveliness, so tiny yet so perfect. Her proud mother was obviously completely smitten and appeared radiant for one who had so shortly undergone the rigours of childbirth. Both Catherine and I could not help but have our hearts melted by the little creature that, as we were bestowing our admiration, began to cry quite heartily. Edythe immediately took the babe to her breast where it suckled eagerly in a bid to sate its obvious hunger. We duly congratulated both parents and left some oatcakes and a small jar of blackberry preserve with Edward. Both thanked us warmly and with that we vacated the property, our spirits mightily lifted by such a wonderful occasion.

I cannot imagine what a mixed blessing it must be to give rise to new life in these inauspicious times. Such joy in being gifted a child, innocent, beautiful and so unaware, yet such dread in the knowledge that it might be taken so cruelly and speedily back from whence it came. I blame not Edythe for her caution; it is a mother's instinct is it not to protect her child by any means possible? God knows we have borne witness to enough having their journey in life cut short upon it barely commencing. May God bless them.

28th January 1666

The village meeting was called today at Cucklett Delf. After lunch we all made our way up for the appointed time. A notice had been pinned upon the church door and word was quickly spread about for those who could not read. It was well attended, only those who are sick or nursing the sick were absent. I stood with Mother, Joseph and Mr. Daniel. We were all well wrapped up against the cold though sheltered somewhat by the large outcrops of limestone on either side.

As I stood there I noticed for the first time that the solitary crag of limestone before me was so honeycombed with caverns that from my vantage point it resembled a huge skull. The dark cavernous eye sockets seemed to stare down at us all there gathered with an empty indifference.

At the head of the delf stood Mr. Stanley and slightly to his right Mr. Mompesson, with Catherine at his shoulder. A table of rock lay just before them forming a natural alter. Our collective chatter was silenced as the reverend raised a hand in address. A fine, strong figure he cut, stood there against the backdrop of stone with the hills just visible above in the distance. His long hair was gathered in by a band at the nape of his neck and some of the loose strands blew about his face in the cold air. His long coat tails flapped at his sides yet his voice could be heard quite clearly by all above the prevailing wind, as it resonated off the rock faces that enclosed us.

The reverend and Mr. Stanley both spoke with such strength of conviction that we could not but listen attentively. They talked at length (Mr. Stanley quoting from the bible on occasion) of our responsibility in keeping the spread of the disease contained within the confines of the village so that it would not spill into neighbouring communities and wreak its havoc and suffering there.

Mr. Mompesson spoke, as always, with much eloquence on how the plague had already taken so much from so many of us, of how it had held us in its grasp and controlled us. It was time now, he urged, for us to take control, to fight back and not let it beleaguer and destroy the lives of those in the surrounding villages, towns and cities. We all, he told us, had through our actions the lives of many others held in our hands. We had the power and the moral responsibility to protect and spare our brothers and sisters from being blighted and afflicted by this evil pestilence. Thus we might all become their saviours as Jesus was ours. We are all one, he continued, and must prevent the harm to others as we would have done for ourselves and our beloved.

He demonstrated how already we have become united by our common experience and our grief, in our caring for the stricken and the grieving, in the sharing of our food and resources and in our many daily acts of kindness. While it was fresh in my mind, directly on my return, I scribbled down some of his words, those that touched me deeply. I will make note of them here.

"First and foremost I welcome all of you here gathered to our new place of worship, it being deemed too dangerous to confine ourselves within the closed walls of our church. Do not despair in this, for I believe that it matters not where we assemble, for God is with us wherever we might be. Seek him not then in a church, on a hillside, in a forest or in your homes, but rather look within yourselves; in your hearts and in your soul, for there He is in residence.

"And ye shall seek me and find me, for ye seek me with all your heart. Jeremiah. Chapter twenty-nine, verse thirteen.

"Be still and know that I am God. Psalm forty-six, verse ten.

"Oft times it is seen that the worst of situations gives rise to the noblest of deeds, out of darkness shines the light that springs forth from our souls. Our highest thoughts are acted upon and are true selves revealed. From the depths of our despair we have risen and on the raising of our downcast eyes we have perceived an opportunity; the unique gift to be who we truly are, to be our highest selves, for the God that dwells in each and every one of us may be now manifested. Alas, if that all people could always be so, what a glorious world we would inhabit.

"I have observed first-hand the transformation that we as a community have undergone. This pestilence is a great leveller, it has no respect for age, gender or standing; in its eyes we are all equal. So we recognise ourselves now as equal, no one life is more important than another, no individual merits special treatment, we all of us merit it. We are no longer focused so on chasing material gain. Envy and jealousy have been vanquished in our bid to survive and hence unveiled before us are the riches of our souls. Acts of love and compassion have become commonplace and perhaps more importantly, we are living with a real understanding of how very precious this gift of life is. We are all constantly living in, and for, the moment. We now understand that that is all there is. We have been forced into a greater and deeper awareness and that is no bad thing.

"I have been glad witness to our transformation. I have witnessed one time enemies helping each other as past disagreements are buried and forgotten, for it is realised that they serve us not. I have witnessed all amongst us selflessly nursing and caring for the afflicted with little or no care for our own well-being, for this we know to be the right course of action. I have witnessed the men amongst us spending more time at home with their families and less hours spent frivolously in the taverns, for this we realise is what really matters to us and, I have witnessed a great generosity in the sharing of all we have amongst those in need, for this is the realisation that we are all one. In this time that tries our souls and burdens our hearts, this has been my strength. By your actions my despondent spirit is lifted, by your actions my faith remains consistent, each of you here and those who are absent, for at this moment they are nursing their loved ones, all of you are my inspiration and for that I thank each and every one of you with all of my heart.

"We know now that whatever hardships and atrocities we face we are not alone, for God is always with us in our hearts, in our souls and in our minds. We grieve for our loved ones but are comforted in the knowledge that they cannot die, their souls have merely returned home from whence they came, for they are not only with God but are one with God, with all that is. God knows who we truly are. He is the truth that lies within all our souls and doubt not that he delights in us knowing and realising our truth. Let us then continue to work selflessly together as one. Let us continue to love and care for every man, woman and child. In comforting them we find comfort; their joys are our joys and their pains and sufferings likewise are our own. Let us live in unity, as one, and may God bless each and every one of us. Amen."

As the reverend stepped away there was a moment of silence. It was our own Mr. Daniel who first then put his hands together in applause and thereafter he was joined by all. I looked around. Some had smiles upon their faces, some had a look of new determination, some of inspiration and some gently wiped the tears from their eyes. I was struck at that moment by all we had achieved together, the strength and resilience each one of us had shown and my heart filled with love and pride for each and every one of us and in that moment I felt a unity, that 'oneness' of us all.

Mr. Stanley then stepped forward.

"Before I start upon the practicalities, on behalf of us all I would like to thank the reverend for his speech. We are all I think deeply moved.

Let it be known that I have spent many hours in theological dialogue with Mr. Mompesson and although we disagree on many aspects of our faith, we have reached an acceptance of those differences and indeed have harboured a profound mutual respect. Now is not the time to argue over 'details', now is the time to put the fundamental principles of what we know to be right into practise. We have discussed and worked together for many an hour and we would now like to put forward to you the following proposals that, if agreed to and adhered to by all, would, we believe, make us act in accordance with His teachings and become ourselves saviours of our fellow man.

"Firstly, white crosses must continue to be daubed upon any homestead visited, such that others may be warned of the infection held therein. We must bury our dead in our gardens, orchards and fields, as soon as possible after death, and in graves no less than six feet deep. If necessary we must bury our own. If the ground be too hard to excavate, the dead will be put to rest at Shepherd's Flatt in Mr. Morton's barn, it being the furthest building from any other, until such a time as the graves are able to be made ready. There will be no more services held for the deceased at church, but a blessing will be given by myself or the good reverend upon the deathbed or as soon after as is possible.

"Secondly, the church doors will be locked from here forth and all services will be held here at the delf instead. Service will be given on a Wednesday, Friday and two upon the Sabbath. The congregation are to stand in family units at least twelve feet apart from one another to prevent the risk of contagion.

"Finally, no one is to leave or enter the village. It has been arranged with the Earl of Devonshire that money will be left upon the boundary stone in holes filled with vinegar in exchange for food, medicines and any other provisions deemed necessary. The Earl has kindly offered to supply the above at half the normal value due to the unfortunate circumstances in which we find ourselves and should our affliction, God forbid, continue so that all monies are spent, he has given his word that he will see no one starve.

"I would like to finish by quoting John fifteen verse thirteen. It is there stated clearly:

'Greater love hath no man than this, that he lay down his life for his friends.' May God bless each and every one of us. Amen."

In short then, we are to cut ourselves off completely from the outside world. We all, I think, saw sense in these words and the righteousness of the proposed actions. In any case, most families who have the means to leave and relatives open enough of heart to accept them, have already long since departed. All of course except those who stood before us today, the good reverend and his wife and Mr. Stanley. They have elected instead to risk their own lives in comforting and nursing others; all the more reason then that we felt disinclined to refute them.

Mr. Howe was the only person to break the silence, putting up some objection along the lines of not being prisoner to anything nor anyone. His wife, having a little more sense and looking somewhat ashamed, placed her hand upon his arm, upon which he was quietened directly. The rest of us were subdued in our reaction, silent in our reflection. We all knew deep in our hearts that the words spoken today were born of notions worthy and true. The proposals must be met for the sake of those of us that remain, for the sake of those lost to us and for the sake of all mankind, that no more should suffer and endure what we, gathered upon that hillside, have been made to suffer and endure. It was nigh on an hour and a half later that we began slowly to depart, our hearts held within them a heavy burden yet into our spirits crept a feeling of unification, of oneness bought about through a shared purpose and in with it crept also, strangely, small seeds of hope, sentiments many of us had little experienced of late. On dispersing, the gazes of others were met, smiles were exchanged and heads nodded in silent assertion.

God bless: Robert Rowbotham, Samuel Rowbotham, Abel Rowland, John Thornley, Isaac Wilson.

3rd February 1666

It has been almost a week now since the meeting was called at Cucklett Delf. There has been a rota made for the depositing of coins and picking up of goods from the appointed collection sites. It seems to be working well so far and the Earl has stayed true to his word, indeed it is said by all how generous he has been in his provision. Mr. Howe, it seems, has not been so generous in his opinion and has been heard to remark with scepticism that the Earl's generosity is born from ensuring that his own life be put not at peril. Fortunately most are used to Mr. Howe's mean-spirited nature and so take little notice of such examples of his ungrateful dissuasion.

Catherine says that Mr. Mompesson is well pleased by the reaction of the villagers and talks of their unrivalled strength of character and sense of moral responsibility. Mr. Stanley and he are meeting most days to compile lists of medicines, comestibles and any other provisions considered requisite. Catherine and I continue to produce batches of plague water and poultices in the hope of alleviating the suffering of those ailing. Upon my journey to the rectory this morning I noticed that a white cross had been painted upon the Morten's door. It sent a shiver down my spine to see this daubed symbol of condemnation, though used not for the first time, it being now considered and officially recognised as a kind of pronunciation of the tragic acts of demise being played out within those walls.

The Earl, acquired from his physician, has provided us new recipes that might be effective against the symptoms of plague. He has also packaged the required ingredients. Catherine and I attempted this morning to produce some of the suggested remedies.

For the first we took three gills of the best Malmsey which we boiled 'til one pint were boiled away. To this we added a long pepper, ginger and nutmegs which were all beaten. We left it to boil again and then put in one ounce of Venice treacle and a quarter pint of aqua vitae. One spoonful of the solution needs to be taken morning and evening.

Next we prepared a poultice recipe for the placing on of sores. We mixed rye meal and bay salt together with the yolks of eggs to make a paste. It is stated that the paste must then be spread upon a piece of leather and applied to the sore or carbuncle. This apparently should draw the poison to the centre so that the sore should then ripen and break away. We then read that to expediate the cure of the infection when it is broke, the rump of a live chicken or toad should be placed upon the open mouth of the sore. This I have heard rumour of before. The poor animal will then, it is said, draw the poison out and into its own body, upon doing so it will perish. This is to be repeated until finally the animal survives, thus indicating that the poison is exhausted and the patient be in a very fair way of recovering health! It is added that the toad might be more efficacious if dried first; there was also a warning on the bottom of the sheet that on occasion the poor beast might explode!

Catherine and I agreed that when delivering the poultice we would pass on the instructions given referencing the use of live creatures but would neither deliver nor oversee their delivery ourselves. We hold out hope that these new remedies might be to some effect, however, there are few so far who have recovered from this awful malady.

Marshall Howe is one who was stricken in the disease's early days but who has since made a return to full health. Many believe that due to his build, resembling that of an ox and his gargantuan height, he was successful in vanquishing the scourge from his body. Although it seems a mere handful overcome and the vast majority alas succumb, we cannot though be seen to give up hope, for then we are all surely doomed.

Mr. Mompesson, it seems, has received a letter from Mrs. Bagshaw enquiring as to the state of her affairs here in Eyam. Catherine found it quite by chance whilst sweeping out the hearth; it had been crumpled into a small ball and thrown there. Not recognising the handwriting, Catherine smoothed it out as best she could fearing it might be of some importance and was lying strewn there by some accident. On deciphering the signature at the bottom, she allowed her own curiosity to get the better of her and began hurriedly to read a few of the pages.

It appears that Mrs. Bagshaw and her daughter, Ann, are quite comfortably installed with their relatives in Manchester. The aforementioned relatives cannot, it seems, do enough for the two ladies and they have been wholly enjoying the numerous parties and gatherings held, the likes of which they have never before encountered: the variety of food and drink being quite beyond their realms of expectation. Indeed, the kindly relatives are now busily employed in trying to find them suitable accommodation of their own. Unfortunately, none has met as yet entirely with Mrs. Bagshaw's approval. However, undeterred, they continue their search tirelessly and her hosts, she states, have even been so benevolent as to offer to provide financial assistance, so that a property considered to be befitting by herself and her daughter might soon be secured. A sign she remarks, as to the esteem in which they are both held!

So amusing was Catherine's recounted version of the letter that I wickedly begged her to retrieve it so that I might read it for myself. Unfortunately, in an attack of conscience, she threw it back upon the hearth and hastily placed upon it some kindling and coal which she then set alight to warm some water with which Mr. Mompesson might wash upon his return.

This afternoon I walked up to the village boundary to meet Rowland. He was sat huddled upon the fallen sycamore branch eating the remains of his lunch. He turned to wave and I held up three fingers to show him all was well. We stood there for some minutes staring at each other. I tried to make out the details of his face from the distance between us. In my mind's eye I saw the mole just above his lip on the right side, his hair at the temples slightly greying at the roots and how his eyebrows arched into slight points in the middle. How I wished to hold that face in my hands and to inhale the familiar smell of his warm skin. I stayed until my feet felt like ice and my hands were blue with cold, then we waved and turned our backs upon future's frail promise to recommence our separate lives.

Upon entering the house I found Mother not in the kitchen, as is usual for this hour, but instead out in the back garden. Mr. Daniel had bought one of his hens and a cockerel for us to keep. He has constructed a run and small house for them against the back wall so they might be safe from any foxes. Mother is delighted, being a farmer's daughter she has always pined for some animals to keep. This evening we laid their house with a bed of straw and threw the vegetable peelings from supper into the enclosure. We then watched as they feasted upon them. Before bed, Mother sat planning how best to put the eggs to use. It is the first time in many months that I have seen her so animated and daring to contemplate and make ready for days to come. Joseph too is much pleased by the new additions to our family and when picked up, points to the back door in the hope of us following his finger into the back garden and across to the hen house. The poor mite becomes most agitated and discordant when we ignore his request!

Both the Rowlands and the Wilsons are now visited. It is feared the Wilson family were infected by the Rowlands, Abel and Isaac being firm friends since childhood. Isaac Wilson had visited Abel during his confinement and inadvertently contracted the disease himself. He had been helping his father, Thomas, to nurse his only son, the mother Mary, having passed on the first day of December. So unjust it seems when such acts of selfless kindness turn out to be of fatal consequence.

12th February 1666

Many households are now visited simultaneously. It appears that over the past week or so the disease has suddenly developed new vigour. White crosses have appeared upon the doors of the Rowland's and the Wilsons'. It is told that we have a self-appointed plague sexton in the guise of Mr. Howe. His new occupation suits him well for he lends a frightening figure with his broad cheekbones and dark, penetrating, deep-set eyes that lie partly obscured below the dense bush of his brows. It is said he is to be seen in the dead of night dragging bodies by their heels to the Miner's Croft or to the common land behind the church, where upon he hastily digs out their final resting place and unceremoniously deposits them therein. His stature and thick set shoulders, I imagine, would indeed lend themselves well to such a task.

Mr. Howe may be called upon it seems, for a small fee, by anyone who has neither the courage nor the strength to bury their own. If it happens that the last survivor of a household perish, he will willingly go and dispose of the corpse. Catherine tells me that he has expressed to Mr. Mompesson his belief that he is immune from infection, he being stricken in the first weeks and having thereafter made a complete recovery. What a grim task he has taken upon himself to perform. Though arguably deemed necessary, I cannot imagine what might drive him to undertake such a miserable and wretched deed.

The plague sexton is now a frequent visitor to the rectory, much to Catherine's disdain, as he has given his word to report the burial of each and every one of his kinsmen to Mr. Mompesson. Catherine does battle with herself, for though she tries to find good in everyone as is her Christian nature, she admits that in Mr. Howe she has yet to discover a redeeming feature. Indeed, she has taken to hiding in the larder upon his arrival, so strong is her fear and loathing of him. Though she knows she is being quite illogical, she claims that he is followed everywhere by the sickly stench of death and that after he has taken his leave, she is obliged to burn clumps of rosemary in an attempt to eradicate the foul-smelling trail that is left in his wake.

Mr. Stanley, on his visits with Mr. Mompesson, has been elected to take down the last wills and testaments of those who are near their life's end, before giving their blessing. Both men being so highly respected, erudite and well-trusted, despite their difference in age and religious views, have bonded together in a single purpose; that of relieving, as far as is possible, any discomfort or anxiety harboured by those who are unfortunate enough to find themselves in their final hours. The reverend conducts last rites and grants absolution so that they might have peace of mind in passing, whilst Mr. Stanley puts their more earthly concerns in order, thus affording them the assurance that there will be no confusion arising as to the state of their affairs and the distribution thereof, subsequent to their death.

The pestilence, being so virile of late, has ensued in Mr. Mompesson and Mr. Stanley being relentless in their rounds. They often pass whole nights with neither rest nor slumber. Catherine says that the reverend now snatches at sleep and meals as and when he can, and there is never much pause between the seemingly incessant raps upon the rectory door, calling him to duty at all hours of the day and night.

Catherine and I continue to keep house and ensure that there is always warm food and water at hand for whenever it might be needed. Sometimes of an evening, especially if Mr. Daniel has occasion to call upon Mother, I will keep Catherine company for an hour or so at the rectory, for I know how she hates to be there alone, particularly after dark. We pass the time in conversation, in reading together or in me listening to her playing of the clavichord, the music giving rise to reveries, some sweet some melancholic in nature. Oft times she will read me the latest correspondence received from her dear relations in Sheffield, detailing news of her beloved children.

I know how eagerly she awaits these letters. I have often witnessed her in the morning, running to the door as the packages of food and provisions are delivered, rummaging immediately through the bag which contains any correspondences, hoping to catch a glimpse of that familiar handwriting upon envelope. So greedy is she for news of them that the seal is broken upon the spot and she is already halfway through the first page on re-entering the kitchen. So deeply engrossed is she then that I let her sit, digesting in silence, as I warm some milk, for I know she will be glad of it during the second, third and oft times even forth reading.

How I wish that I had taught Rowland to write so that I too might have such precious words to keep and to reread when in need of strength. At least I am able to set eyes upon him. Alas, poor Catherine cannot witness for herself how her babes are changed.

20th February 1666

Mother and I followed the now well-trodden path that meanders out of the village, descends the steep slopes of the valley, crosses the small rivulet that runs from the gorge and climbs the grassy knoll that leads to the delf. Here, some having bought blankets in which to wrap themselves, we sat upon the grassy slopes with a good distance between us and partook of the Sabbath service. Each week the reverend's flock is more diminished. Three new households are daubed with the white cross: The Hawkesworths, the Blackwalls and the Abells. As I look around I am sure I am not alone in wondering who next amongst us is to be affected.

I have now become quite used to our new place of worship. Indeed, I feel closer there to God than ever I did in the gloom of our man-made, stone church. Mr. Mompesson conducts his sermons from the arched cavern, more resplendent a pulpit, I doubt, is to be found in any church in the country. For where is God more present than in the beauty of the rolling hills so soft and green, or in the endless stretch of sky above with its slow moving clouds and hurrying birds? He is there in the calm, the still and the constant which has been here for thousands of years before us and which will stay yet for thousands more after we are gone.

I feel God to be at my side constantly now. I recognise His hand in all that surrounds me, odd though that might seem given our circumstance, moreover is it surely not because of it? Before, I communicated with God only at church or bedtime prayers. I sought Him in moments of extreme sadness, hardship or joy. Now I feel myself to be in almost consistent communion with Him. Before, as a member of the congregation, I listened carefully and tried to make sense of the preacher's lengthy sermons, or of the passages read from the Bible, so that I might know Him better. Now in moments of quiet contemplation I look as well to my soul and there I always find Him.

It seems quite naïve of me now; looking meticulously at isolated segments, I merely succeeded in obscuring the reality of the whole. It is as when the whole of a room is obscured when focused on trying to pass a length of thread through the eye of a needle. My confusion it seems was in my over complication of something which was in fact most simple. I was too busy searching and questioning when all I needed it seems, was to be still and listen.

27th February 1666

When at the rectory this morning a most peculiar incident was related to us by Mr. Mompesson. It appears that our self-appointed sexton, Mr. Howe, has taken to burying the living as well as the dead!

The tale Mr. Mompesson recounted went thus: The eve before last Mr. Howe is informed that the body of a man has been found in the bedroom of his home at 'The Town Head'. Mr. Howe immediately collects up his spade and hastens to the orchard to the rear of the house in order to dig the grave. Once the task is completed he enters the victim's home and taking a sheet from upon one of the beds, he proceeds to tie it around the deceased's ankles. Once secured, Mr. Howe begins to drag the corpse carelessly down the stairwell. It is then that the dead man suddenly lets out a cry and amidst much blaspheming, orders the startled Mr. Howe to let off and fetch him a posset. Mr. Howe, terrified and with a pallor to match that of one of his unfortunate clients, dumps the body without further ado and makes a swift exit.

The poor man, who was unwittingly nigh committed to the earth alive, was Unwinn. He being infamous for his love of drink and oft times being found senseless under the curse of alcohol. He had, that evening, collapsed due to inebriation rather than as was first assumed, through having met his demise at the hands of the pestilence, and save for a few bumps and bruises is now quite recovered. The village it seems is at present full of the story and all mockingly raise a glass to the miraculous revival of Unwinn! What a pleasant change indeed it must make to be raising a glass to the living rather than to the dead.

This afternoon I went again to meet Rowland. On reaching the boundary stone I held up three fingers as usual, to indicate that all was well. Upon so doing I believe I could just discern the smile that lifted his cheeks. Last week he left a freshly killed rabbit at the stone for me to take for Mother, Joseph and I. By sign I had to demonstrate that I could not accept his kind offer, for how would I explain its procurement to Mother? None in the village, however, are short of food or any kind of provisions as the Earl has stayed true to his word and we have plentiful supplies of all that is requested. We have received news from Chatsworth House that thus far our efforts to contain the disease have been successful, for it seems no one in the surrounding villages has as yet been infected.

God bless: Peter Morton, Thomas Rowland, John Wilson, Deborah Wilson, Alice Wilson, Adam Hawkesworth, Anthony Blackwall, Elizabeth Abell.

2nd March 1666

Mr. Daniel's visits have become more frequent. Today on my return from my meeting with Rowland, I found him seated in the kitchen with Mother and Joseph. Though not impolite he is a man not given naturally to communication and oft times seems ill at ease in my presence. I therefore normally tend to retire to my room. This afternoon, however, I needed to attend to the preparation of a potage for supper, us having finished the one made earlier in the week last evening.

With the provision of some root vegetables and pulses, I put our large cooking pot upon the hearth and proceeded in the preparation of the repast. Aware of the uncomfortable silence that dominated the room, I attempted to engage Mother and Mr. Daniel in conversation. I talked of my duties at the rectory and of Catherine's relentless energy and kindness in the calling upon the sick and grieving, whilst herself suffering from the absence of her own children so acutely. Mother, relieved by my efforts, began to make enquiries as to the well-being of little George and Elizabeth. Mr. Daniel meanwhile amused young

Joseph by spinning his wooden top before him as he sat upon the floor. Joseph issued noises of delight and was apparently enjoying the attention. After a time Mr. Daniel, obviously feeling a little more relaxed, spoke soft words of encouragement as he played with him. Indeed, as the afternoon progressed the atmosphere transformed itself into one of easiness and so we all began to interject more naturally and freely.

Mr. Daniel talked tenderly of his wife and their sadness at not having been able to parent children of their own, the first-born having exited this world only two days after its arrival. I was touched by his words and impressed by his honesty and frankness - men not usually being given to such characteristics. It struck me then that he was as effeminate in nature as he was in physique, being of a slight build, slender of hip and narrow of shoulder. His pale complexion and long, fair hair could even, I imagine, incite the envy of many a young woman.

As I went about my business I occasionally caught them in the exchange of a tender look or understanding smile and, though it shocked me rather, somewhere deep in the core of my being it also warmed my heart to see these demonstrations of affection. I could not, however, help myself in comparing him to Father. How different they were in both looks and character! Though a just and fair man, my father cut a rather dark and brooding figure. He also was not given to conversation, not through any self-consciousness or insecurity but rather through ill-temper, his utterances being often curt and belying a shortness of patience. On few occasions did I witness any tenderness or indeed much interest displayed towards his children. Mother always attributed his sternness and ill-humour to the hard nature of his labour at the mines. Indeed, as if to defend his shortcomings she would often describe him to us as she remembered him in his youth: an optimistic young man who was a bit of a dreamer, having as he did grand designs upon their future together.

Mr. Daniel did not strike me as a dreamer, being so practical as he was in nature. There was not much that he could not repair, fix or improve upon and we had already benefited greatly from his capabilities as regards both the house and garden. Towards the end of the afternoon he accompanied Joseph into the backyard to see the hen and cockerel. He let Joseph take hold of his two index fingers and patiently followed behind his tentative steps. Upon his departure, as if having read my thoughts, Mother quietly declared,

"I know he is not your father Emmott, but he is of good heart."

Knowing not quite how to reply I merely nodded in agreement, upon which Mother turned her attention to the setting of the table.

Mr. Daniel took supper with us. After, I took Joseph up and settled him upon his mattress. As I write this I am able to hear the soft murmurings of Mr. Daniel and my mother in conversation rising from the room below. I am used now to falling asleep with this noise as my backdrop. It is comforting to know that Mother is well and cared for. I drift away more swiftly and peaceably.

5th March 1666

Marshall Howe, our self-appointed sexton, had the miserable task of burying his wife and only child this week. On two successive nights he was seen digging out their graves in his own back garden, howling all the while it is said like 'a wounded hound'.

On our walk this afternoon, Catherine relayed how he had confessed to the rector that his wife and son had been taken from him in payment for his sins. Indeed, it has long been rumoured that Mr. Howe has been claiming his own payment for his deeds from those he has interred. Just a fortnight or so ago was he heard blatantly boasting in 'The Miner's Arms' that he had 'Pinners and napkins enough to kindle the pipe' whilst he lives.

Catherine, through the crack in the parlour door, witnessed Mr. Howe upon his knees, hat in hand before her husband. She heard him make a promise to Mr. Mompesson that from this day forth he would carry out his self-imposed duties correctly and honestly. Dolefully, between stifled sobs, he expressed his belief of how the pestilence was brought to his door, nestled amidst the wrongfully acquired goods of the deceased and borne across the threshold in his own arms.

So pained and wretched did he appear that Catherine could not help but feel a pity for him take root in her heart. As he left, hat in hand, his gigantic frame seemed somewhat shrunken by grief, his shoulders hung low and his feet dragged heavily across the floor. Upon his departure

Catherine, feeling quite repentant in her harsh judgement of him prior, pressed a meat pie wrapped in a square of muslin into his hands. On doing so she could not help but notice the unusual length and breadth of his fingers, behind the nails of which were harboured lines of dried earth, and the enormous width of his palms, covered as they were in calluses born of his woeful labours. He regarded her from beneath his unkempt brows with eyes that brimmed with tears and in a voice broken by grief, thanked her awkwardly for her kindness and then shuffled towards the door. Catherine held it open to see him out and just as she was shutting it behind him he turned, and in a tone more akin to enquiry than appeal, she heard him usher the words, "May God forgive me?"

In times of extremes such as these, it seems that the true nature of those we have grown up with, of those we have lived in close proximity to, is revealed to us and more frighteningly it seems, to their selves. There is no way of knowing who the monsters may be amongst us, who the cowards and who the heroes. We may only hope that we might know our own soul, but until we stand face-to-face with our own immortality there can be no certainty. Situations such as warring, pestilence, drought and starvation; when the parameters of normality dissipate and we find our very existence threatened, that is when the strengths and weaknesses of our soul are laid bare.

12th March 1666

Catherine and I have spent most of the day at the rectory. We have, it appears, a respite to the onslaught. We prepared the poultices and then went about the sorting of food parcels to be distributed. As I was making ready the bundles, Catherine produced an envelope from her apron skirt.

"It's from the Bagshaws," she proclaimed with a slight glint in her eyes. "I found it discarded in the study waste bin and as the last amused you so, I decided to keep it especially for your perusal!"

Glad for a break from our chores, I sat expectantly at the parlour table as Catherine handed me the correspondence. I began to read it aloud, attempting to the best of my abilities to mimic Mrs. Bagshaw's voice and intonation. This amused Catherine verily and the both of us succumbed to frequent fits of laughter, so much so that on completion the muscles of our stomachs ached and we were wiping the tears from our eyes. Such were we when Mr. Mompesson entered unexpectedly.

"How wonderful to hear such laughter," He announced. "So ladies, please do tell, what entertains you so?"

I hastily stuffed the letter and envelope under my apron and into the folds of my skirts as we gathered our composure.

"Oh it is nothing William," explained Catherine. "Emmott and I were just recalling the incident of the hog that escaped up on the Talbot's this summer gone."

"Ah yes indeed. Poor Mr. Talbot was by all accounts quite shaken up by the incident. Mind you, I have heard it told before that such beasts can become rather aggressive. Indeed, it is told that they are relatively intelligent creatures. Have you by chance seen my cloth coat Catherine? I thought I might pay a visit to Unwinn. It has been a while since I or anyone else has received news of him. Oh and Emmott, here is a letter that was in a correspondence from Mrs. Bagshaw. You are entrusted, I believe, to pass it on to young Edythe Taylor."

Whilst Catherine replied that indeed, she had remarked this morning that her husband's coat was hung behind the study door, I placed the envelope that Mr. Mompesson had forwarded me into the folds of my underskirt along with the previous. Upon which Mr. Mompesson bid us farewell and departed.

It must be here said that this was the first time I have known Catherine to tell an untruth, yet from her agile response and the naturalness of her demeanour in doing so, one would be forgiven for judging it to be a common occurrence.

I began then to inquire as to Mr. Mompesson's specific interest in Unwinn, for it is told that he frequents his abode on quite a regular basis. Catherine was surprised to learn that I knew very little of his history.

It is common knowledge that he has access to funds from some source unknown, for he is rarely in work and yet has always enough income to sate his abundant appetite for alcohol, he being more often drunk than he is sober. Indeed oft times, I have heard tell, is he known to stand rounds for all others present, such is his generosity. This said, strangely he has few friends and engages little in conversation with any man, preferring rather to keep his thoughts, opinions and history to himself.

I had known also that he had happened upon Eyam as a young man whilst affiliated to a group of players one Wakes' tide many years hence. My understanding was that he became tired of the players' circuit and decided to stay in Eyam, it being as good a place as any, whilst the rest of the band continued on their journeying.

I had also heard many rumours as to his character; some spoke of a clandestine lover and described spying a 'grand lady' through his half-shuttered windows. An alternative version to this tale was that the 'grand lady' was rather a wench of ill-repute brought by horse and carriage from a neighbouring town, hired out on occasion for the night. Others told that he had a rich lady relative who visited in secret, so ashamed was she of his abased social status.

"'Tis a sad story Emmott and one I trust that if shared with you will go no further."

I gave her my word which I will hold to my dying day, but I consider it a shame that more are not aware, for they too would have a greater understanding of the man he has become. Though it was obvious on my hearing as to why he has trusted very few with his story.

Unwinn, she related, was indeed a member of a group of players that travelled the county and beyond providing entertainment during any festivities that might demand them. Usually this would entail a short theatrical piece with songs accompanied by a small band of instruments. I have seen such groups in our own village on many an occasion. Unwinn, it seems, was the comedian of such a group. Whilst unable to hold a note or play an instrument, he had, it is told, a gift to elicit laughter from young and old alike. There being no women in such groups, Unwinn would take on the part of any female and so clever were his exaggerations of the fairer sex that they always provoked amusement amongst his audience. The louder the crowd afore gathered laughed, the more exaggerated became his performances. He took even to making his own costumes for such roles and drew great satisfaction from their creation.

After a while, his fellow players began to remark how they had caught him in costume when not performing. Indeed, as time progressed he was noted to be more in costume than out of it. A few of the other group members began to unkindly tease and taunt him for this. Apparently it was at this time that Unwinn began to consume more ale and mead then was deemed wise. Soon his drinking grew to be beyond the bounds of control; though still attached to his group of players he performed rarely and when he did so, his characters were deemed to have become more grotesque than comical. Oft times he would not perform at all and instead drink himself into a stupor behind the makeshift stage, slopped clumsily against one of the panels, with his make-up on and still in costume. Naturally, the players decided they could carry him no longer so after a performance, here upon the village green, they stole away leaving him propped against the trunk of a tree, inebriated and unconscious. So it is that he came to reside in Eyam.

Catherine tells me that oft times when her husband calls upon him he is wearing one of his beloved costumes, sometimes with painted face and wig too. It is only when he ventures into the village that he changes them for pants and shirt. Catherine says he is a poor tormented soul and sadly I must concur.

Upon undressing this evening, the envelope and letter fell from the folds of my skirt. I will attach it upon the next page for it has been a long while since I have experienced such mirth. It will be a reminder!

Manchester.

24th February 166

My Dearest Reverend,

I hope most sincerely that my correspondence finds your dear self and your respectful family in the best of health. News has recently reached us here in Manchester of your self-induced 'cordon sanitaire', and I could no longer refrain from writing to congratulate the village, no doubt under your persuasion, of its selfless undertaking.

Only last Sunday did I converse with my own dear reverend upon the topic and we had to concur that such an act of faith and manifestation of Christian value; the sacrifice of your own for the well-being of others (such as Ann and myself), would be hard to surpass. Indeed, we are now most proud to be connected to the village and when we hear the name of 'Eyam' mentioned in conversation as it is, let me assure you, on many occasions being quite the 'sujet de maintenant', we are at once compelled to step forward and reveal it as our own rural residence. In so doing we immediately attract no end of interest and find we are quite the centre of attention most everywhere we go!

I am in no doubt that you will be glad to hear that dearest Ann and my good self are most comfortably installed in a rather grand establishment in the most exclusive district of the city, found and organised for us by our generous friends, Mr. and Mrs. Cuthbert. Indeed, they even went so far as to arrange the removal and transfer of the few possessions we managed to abscond with. Which, my dear reverend, brings me to the subject at hand. We are, Ann and I, as you might imagine, quite desperate to have a few of our personal belongings transported to our new abode. I cannot help but reflect on how grand the sideboard in the hall might look installed in our lounge, or the armchair in the study here by the fire etc. etc. So we were wondering whether you might be so good as to arrange the conveyance of certain items, that is, once the 'cordon sanitaire' is lifted, naturally. If in agreement, I will have sent a list of our vital necessities and of course, our full address for the careful delivery thereof.

As you might well have inferred Ann and I are regular and devoted members of the local church here where, I am pleased to say, we have made the acquaintance of many like-minded gentry. Indeed, it affords us quite a large social sphere and we have been fortunate enough to have received invites to many a gathering, the likes of which could only be imagined at in dear Eyam.

The tables are laid with china plates and silver cutlery and candelabras which, being so highly-polished, gleam and glisten in the flickering candlelight. Food from across the seas is very much 'en mode' here, flavoured with spices from exotic places, (I must admit I myself, suffering from a rather sensitive constitution, am not too enamoured) but nonetheless one cannot fail to be impressed by the organisation and distance undertaken for it to appear, served thus, on a silver platter before us. The crystal glasses are filled and filled again with fine wines from Europe. Ann and I, of course, do not partake of the alcoholic beverages offered as I consider it to be most unchristian in behaviour. I must concede I am always quite glad of the fact as I witness, during the course of the evening, voices rising in octave and fits of silly girlish giggles emanating from the normally more respected members of our little circle.

Strangely we have seen little of the Cuthberts since the move. I have attempted on several occasions to arrange a 'rendezvous' but regrettably they always seem to be otherwise engaged. In fact I do believe, upon reflection, that we have had the pleasure of seeing them only once since our departure, that being on the occasion they reclaimed the spare key entrusted to us upon our first arrival in Manchester. They are *unfortunately not members of our congregation, the establishment they secured us, belonging as it does, to a different parish. However, in all honesty it suits us much better here, their own church being a lot less ornate and offering a rather more subdued atmosphere altogether.*

Well my dear Reverend, I could continue 'ad infinitum' with my discourse on our rather mundane existence here in the city, however, Ann and I have started to undertake instruction in the French language and our young instructor, who I believe is most fond of our dear Ann, is expected upon the hour.

I await your instruction with regard to the transportation of furniture from Bagshaw Hall.

You and your family are ever in our prayers, may God see fit to reward the righteous!

Dear Ann sends her best regards.

Yours in anticipation,

Mrs. Bagshaw.

14th March 1666

It was with great sadness that Catherine and I learnt from Mr. Mompesson that Elizabeth Blackwell had been taken with distemper. Herself and her brother being the only survivors in their household, we packed Catherine's basket with the usual supplies of medicines and comestibles and made haste to their cottage. Reaching the Blackwell's abode we exchanged hurried concerns with Elizabeth's elder brother Francis, who was on his way out being obliged to make a visit to the coal pit.

"I fear she may pass before my return," he called over his shoulder as he hastened through the gate.

We continued our way up the narrow garden path, clumps of snowdrops huddled under the canopy of a small beech tree and the long, green stems of daffodils could be seen bunched in the grass. The front door had been left unlatched and on entering the kitchen we were welcomed by the smell of recently cooked ham. Indeed, on the table was laid a crust of bread and the white smears of recently congealed lard. A small wooden piggin stood on the edge of the hearth filled with hot liquid fat. The smell made the pit of my stomach moan, for there is nothing quite as effective as the smell of recently cooked, thick slabs of cured bacon to entice hunger. This was immediately abated however, as we mounted the stairs and another, more familiar odour entered my nostrils: that of rotting flesh and vile putrid toxins; the sickly stench of pestilence.

We found that Elizabeth's brother had spoken true for the poor girl was lost in fever and in a delirious sleep. Catherine wiped her brow and laid her out comfortably, straightening her bed clothes and plumping her pillow. Finding there was nothing more to be done, I took back the plague water and poultice, both of which I had placed upon the small and crudely fashioned bedside table, in readiness to administer. We then said a prayer over her and as Catherine blessed her, an image of the four of them: Elizabeth, the two Talbot girls, Bridget and Mary and our own dear Elizabeth, dancing at the Wakes' tide festival, came to my mind. So young, beautiful and carefree were they as they spun one another around, omitting screams of delight and laughter. At only nineteen years of age, as they were then, all were a picture of youth and health with the promise of a future stretching before them. What contrast to this scene of death and decay, of agony and misery, of futures stolen. Sadly resigned, we quietly vacated the property, for we considered her condition too advanced for us to be of any further use. Catherine thought it best to return immediately to the rectory and ask her husband to come directly to administer last rites and wait upon her brother's homecoming. Upon our departure Catherine left a couple of the oatcakes we had made that morning upon the kitchen table, thinking that Francis might appreciate them upon his return.

It was a little after lunch that Catherine and I were returning from making a visit to the Wilsons when we once again happened to cross paths with Elizabeth's brother, Francis. He seemed a little dazed and confused and so fearing the worst, we enquired as to how his sister might fare, to which he answered that upon his return to the house instead of finding her in the final throes of death, or worst cold and lifeless as he had expected, she was sat upright at the kitchen table declaring that she felt herself to be much recovered.

Apparently she was awoken from her feverish slumber by an overwhelming thirst which many suffer as a symptom of this affliction. Half-delirious and with blurred vision, for she tells of her sight being affected too, she managed to stumble to the kitchen where, in her haste to quench the awful thirst which consumed her, she grabbed the wooden piggin and mistaking the liquid fat for warm milk she greedily drank the entire contents. This in turn caused her to vomit violently, whereupon she began to feel much improved, her senses regained and her fever diminished.

We were then invited into the house to witness this miracle for ourselves and were pleasingly dismayed to find Elizabeth, who was, as we can bare testament, but it seemed a few hours from death, sat upright enjoying one of the oatcakes that Catherine had left upon the table on her way out. Although weak and a little shaken, on conversing with her we found her to be both sound of mind and obviously of a much improved physical disposition.

All talk in the village is bound up with this unexpected revival. We are informed that Elizabeth is now up and about and near fully recovered. We are all encouraged and cheered by this small miracle and with many fewer deaths so far this month, we begin to silently hope that the worst has passed.

16th March 1666

Catherine and I distributed the latest bundles of provisions this morning. Our last call was purposefully to the Taylor's house so that we might also hand Edythe the letter entrusted to me. I was of little doubt that Ann had somehow managed to slip it into her mother's correspondence unnoticed before being dispatched.

On entering the small cottage it was truly fortuitous that we found Edythe to be alone with the newborn. Taking advantage, I immediately handed her the envelope, anxious that we might be interrupted at any time. Upon seeing it her frail hand began to tremble and her complexion paled. Hurriedly, she ripped open the seal and unfolded the sheet. For a few moments she stared at the one side then turned it and stared in turn at the other.

"Please Emmott, do read it to me." Her voice trembled slightly.

Obediently I took the page from her and began to recite to her its contents which to my recall went approximately thus:

"My Dearest Edythe,

I can postpone no more my urgency in writing to you. I write this with as much haste as possible, for Mother has entrusted me with the dispatching of her own letter and I must be gone from the house soon. With all of my heart I pray that this letter finds you and that it finds you well. I wonder constantly how you are faring. I know your child must be born now. Every day of the month of January I kept asking myself, 'might it be today?' Strange when I know not whether you be alive or dead. Mother gives me no news of Eyam. Indeed, it is never mentioned when we are without company to impress.

It grieves me so Edythe to have parted in the way we did but it was indeed the imminence of my departure that so incited my frankness of expression. I knew not then, as I know not now, whether indeed I would ever lay my eyes upon you again, and my heart would have rested burdened with regret had I not shared with you its truth.

Edythe, only you have truly known me; what lies within my heart and soul. To all others I have been merely Mrs. Bagshaw's meek and insipid daughter. She who never spoke, for I was always spoken for, she who lacked character and opinion, for my mother's was dominant enough for the both of us. But you knew me as I was in childhood, before the life was sucked from me and in your company it was breathed back into me. Upon the death of my dear father you were my comfort when my mother, so absorbed by the organising of his estate, had no time for me. Through my adolescence it was you alone whom I confided in and conversed with. I love you with every fibre of my being though I always knew my feelings were not to be reciprocated. I could not leave without letting you know it was so.

Your reaction Edythe did not surprise nor disappoint me, expected as it was. I forgave you immediately your harsh words, for in my heart I knew you meant them not. It is my only desire now that I lose not my one and only friend in this world, so if you can forgive me I beg of you to send news of how goes your new life, your marriage and of course, your child. I am at least assured in the knowledge that Edward will be a kind and just husband to you, for I know in what high regard he holds you and that he loves you dearly. In knowing you, who could not?

My life here alone with Mother is one of dreary tedium; I miss your company most terribly. Within the year, Mother would have me married off to a young man who visits once a week to instruct us both in the French language. Mother, as you know, has a habit of always achieving her ends!

Oh Edythe I am sure he is of a pleasant enough disposition but the thought of being joined to him in lifelong union fills me with such dread. He is of average height but most painfully thin and alas he has the most unfortunate of complexions, being covered as he is in angry, red pimples and postulates. It distresses me greatly that this must be my fate, for you know how unnatural a union it would be for me to endure. I do digress and time is a luxury that at present I am ill-afforded.

Please know Edythe that the three of you are in my prayers daily. Take care of yourself my dearest friend and know that I am ever yours.

Ann.

Your reply is both eagerly and anxiously awaited."

I placed the letter upon the table before Edythe, wiping the tears that journeyed down her cheeks she rose and placed the letter upon the top of the pantry cupboard. She then returned and sat opposite, her tear-brimmed eyes staring into mine in earnest.

"Oh, Emmott. I only saw her that once. You know how her mother forbade her any contact and prohibited her from being present at my marriage ceremony, having obviously presumed the condition in which I found myself? I would have it that she had been my only bridesmaid, but alas it was not to be, and for that I am ashamed to say that I was not only bitterly disappointed but taken also with great anger. When Ann came to bid me farewell, I still held much resentment within my heart, though I knew it was her mother's bidding and not her own. Indeed she must have suffered equally, if not more so than myself; her being confined to Bagshaw Hall and being so alone.

"I welcomed her not warmly Emmott. When she began to relate to me her relief at not having to be witness to my marriage, explaining that to have observed me pledging my life and love to another would have been more than she might have borne, I began only then to realise the true nature of her feelings towards me. I was shocked and I am sorry to confess, somewhat repulsed. I felt at that moment that our friendship was betrayed, that it had somehow been all pretence. I gave forth remarks that I now sorely regret.

"You must tell her Emmott. Tell her that my heart is full of love for her and that I feel myself blessed to have received and known such unbending loyalty and companionship. Tell her that I was wrong; that her sentiments were not 'ugly' but a thing of great beauty, pure in their sincerity and intention and indeed, elevated by the uncommonness of their nature. Tell her that I now realise that it is not the direction of love that is important but rather its depth.

"Tell her I am sorry for my unkind words that were uttered in the momentary shock of revelation and have ever since been regretted most profoundly. Tell her Emmott, tell her that I am so, so sorry and though disinclined to share her persuasion, my love for her is as strong as that for my own newborn child. Promise me Emmott, promise me you will tell her."

Thereupon I took her in my arms and did all I might to console her and to reassure her. I promised her that I would write to Ann forthwith and Catherine interjected that she would make sure the letter was dispatched. Once we had managed to calm Edythe sufficiently, we took our leave. On closing the garden gate we exchanged a look of sad surprise.

I told Catherine that I would compose a letter upon the morn, to which she nodded her assent.

18th March 1666

    This is the letter to Ann I scribed today on Edythe's behalf:

Dear Ann,

    I trust this letter finds you well. As instructed by Edythe, who received your letter yesterday, I am writing in reply.

    Firstly, know that Edythe, Edward and their child, Sarah Ann, are all in good health. Sarah Ann came to this world on the eighteenth day of January and was delivered by Edythe's mother, with the help of their neighbour Widow Cooper. Luckily the labour was not protracted and the birth uncomplicated in nature.

    Edythe wishes you to know that she still thinks of you warmly and values your friendship as always. She asked me to tell you that she very much regrets the words she spoke to you upon your last encounter and meant them not. You are as dear to her as always and she harbours only love in her heart for you.

I must explain Ann, that the pestilence inflicted upon us has altered us all in many ways; we are not, and p'raps n'er will be, quite the same. Not only has it taken from us many of our dearly beloved friends and family, but it has also fundamentally changed those of us who remain still. Petty quarrels and rifts are n'er witnessed. We are slower to pass judgement on others and quicker to accept what is. I have noticed a sea change in us all regarding our priorities; we now realise that it is our love and behaviour towards others that is of principal importance, no matter what form that love might take. This said, the esteem and affection held for you by Edythe is not in the slightest diminished but rather it is indeed heightened.

From your letter I ascertain that you have little if no news of the residents of Eyam and hence are ignorant of those unfortunate souls who have fallen victim to the cruel contagion that has decimated our village since your departure. I will list them here though it makes for solemn reading indeed. Upon your leave taking both Alice and Elizabeth were ailing, unfortunately both were lost to us.

Take care of yourself Ann and on behalf of us all I send you our very best wishes. Edythe, of course, sends you much love. She misses you dearly and if providence permits very much hopes to be one day reunited with you.

Kind regards.

Emmott.

October.

Alice Ragge, George Ragge, Jonathan Cooper, Humphrey Torre.

November.

Hugh Stubbs, Alice Teylour, Hannah Rowland, John Stubbs, Ann Stubbs, Elizabeth Warrington, Randoll Danyell.

December.

Jon Rowbotham, Mary and William Rowe's baby, it lasted not a day. Mary Rowe, William Rowe, Thomas Wilson, William Rowbotham, Anthony Blackwall.

January.

Robert Rowbotham, Samuel Rowbotham, Abel Rowland, John Thornley, Isaac Wilson.

February.

Peter Morten, Thomas Rowland, John Wilson, Deborah Wilson, Alice Wilson, Adam Hawkesworth, Anthony Blackwall, Elisabeth Abell.

March.

John Wilson, John Talbot, John Wood, Mary Buxton, Anne Blackwall, Alice Hawkesworth.

20th March 1666

Mother has quite surprised me today by declaring her betrothal to Mr. Daniel. She announced it in a very direct and matter of fact manner, which I know to be her way of dealing with situations in which she finds herself ill at ease. I imagine that she was unsure as to how I might react upon hearing such news. I cannot deny that I found myself silenced momentarily as I absorbed this unexpected proclamation, such was my shock. However, in true Mother-style, I quickly pulled myself together and flung my arms around her, for how could I do otherwise? For she, who having suffered such grief that few on this earth will be hapless enough to have to endure, clings still to hope and desires still happier times.

I was at once amazed and full of admiration for this woman, so slight of build and yet so strong in spirit, who refuses to let life trample upon and destroy her. We held each other tightly and laughed and cried in the same breath. The tears were for those we had loved and lost; the laughter for mankind's ability to overcome and be resurrected, and for love, our salvation.

Joseph sat on the floor and watched in bemusement as his mother and elder sister clung to each other and embraced and danced. Once again this house felt love, laughter and life within its walls as it had oft times done in the past, before all was eclipsed by the shadow of suffering and death. As we held each other tightly, I sensed within me a certainty that those who had loved us dearly, who had once lived here with us but who had now passed, were celebrating with us, encouraging us to continue in unearthing happiness even under the darkest and heaviest of stones. For that is quite simply what love is, a wish for another's happiness, a desire that they find peace.

As I write this I have our ring laid before me. The saying that life is but short has been too oft pressed upon us these last months. All find their solace where they can, in the arms of others, in letters from loved ones, at the bottom of a bottle. Mine is here laid before me, in the promise of a life together, full of our own children and laughter in a time when, with God's will, all this misery is behind us. Like Mother I will not let the cruel hand that fate has dealt us extinguish my love of life or bury completely the seeds of hope that lie dormant in my heart.

God bless: John Wilson, John Talbot, John Wood, Mary Buxton, Anne Blackwall, Alice Hawkesworth.

20th April 1666

Today, Mother and I have been occupied in making preparations for the wedding ceremony. April thus far has been blessed with clear skies and sunshine. We are hoping the weather does not break in the next week as the ceremony is to be held at the delf. This morning we pulled Mother's finest dress from the chest in her room and I took it with me to the rectory, along with some under garments, where Catherine and I carefully laundered and hung them. We were most pleased and congratulated ourselves with the result, it looking so clean that it might have been recently made. Whilst the clothes hung in the afternoon sun to dry, Catherine and I busied ourselves in the collecting of periwinkles which grew shaded at the roots of the large cherry tree. Some we wove and attached in a circle as a garland for Mother's hair, the remainder we tied in a small bundle for her bridal posy.

Catherine has kindly undertaken the preparing and organising of the victuals, which, if fair, will be consumed in the rectory garden. She has baked egg pies and roasted some duck and pigeon and upon her request, the Earl of Devonshire has sent sweetmeats, cake and mead for our refreshment. Within the parcel he included three bottles of the finest wines from his own cellar at Chatsworth House, along with a written card congratulating the newlyweds on their married status and wishing them a long and happy future. As I read it the words struck me as strange:

'a long and happy future' is something none of us villagers nigh dares to think on. The words seemed almost to be tempting fate into raising its cruel sword above our heads, so that it might demonstrate once more who is the stronger.

This evening Mother put on her bridal dress to try. How fine she looked in the pale, green wool, setting off as it did her eyes and the auburn shine to her hair. Thankfully it needed only slight alteration to the waist and bust, being as she is quite diminished through grief. We fastened the garland with some pins Catherine had given me and she held the posy before her. Mother is insisting that her hair be secured for the occasion, claiming that she is too old to wear it loose; no amount of persuading on my part would have her change her mind. A pity I feel, as it hangs so pretty in curls and goes some way towards softening the features that have incurred fine lines and hardened somewhat over this past year.

After I had settled Joseph and Mother had changed out of her dress, we sat 'til late in the parlour. We talked of and shed tears for our loved ones now lost to us. We recalled their habits and foibles with warmth: Sarah's quiet, mature demeanour, Elizabeth's love of life and laughter, Ellen's kind and caring nature, Alice's anxiety and sensitivity, Richard's boisterousness and inquisitiveness and of course, Father, loyal, reliable and steadfast, if a little dour.

Mother wiped away her tears as she took my hand in hers,

"Mr. Daniel is a good man Emmott," she said. "He can turn his hand to most anything and will provide and care well for us...I will grow to love him Emmott, as he loves me."

I squeezed her hand in mine and my thoughts turned to my own Rowland; when we meet how I long to run to him, to be with his arms about me, to feel myself safe in his embrace. How I miss the feel of his rough skin as his large hand wraps itself around my own. As Mother stood in her dress this evening, I could not help but picture myself in the blue bridal gown I have imagined for my own wedding day. The weeks and months pass but it seems an eternity of hoping and waiting and praying. I wear the ring upon my finger now; this evening I am loathed to remove it once again.

26th April 1666

THE WEDDING DAY!

A more temperate day we could not have wished for. We arose early and I assisted Mother in bathing and the washing of her hair. Mother then went upstairs to don her undergarments and skirts. I proceeded to prepare first Joseph then myself. We wore our church outfits as they were all that we possessed befitting the occasion.

I knocked and entered Mother's room, the garland and posy in my hands. I found her sat upon the edge of the mattress, her hands knotted before her, twisting their selves in her lap. I placed the flowers upon the oak chest, she rose slowly and in silence, I pulled on her gown and then proceeded to fasten her hair as instructed. I secured the garland to her head using Catherine's pins and finally, handed her the posy.

The dress somehow disguised her lack of flesh, only the long sleeves which hung loose about her thin arms betrayed the toll that the strain of grief had wreaked upon her now frail body. Indeed, from a distance she appeared just as I remember her in my mind's eye, as she was before the pestilence took a hold of our village, robbed us of our loved ones and made of our former lives a shadow, a mere memory of happier days, as a long winter makes but a hazy memory of the summer past.

We left the house at midday to make our way to the delf. Some had gathered before the cottage to join us. How odd it looked, all gathered in family groups as they were and standing the requisite distance apart. The young girls and women wore spring flowers in their hair, all were attired in their Sunday best. I spotted Elizabeth Blackwell now back to full fitness and radiant in her youth and no doubt, in the knowledge that she had been spared. Mary and Bridget Talbot were present with their family. Some onlookers had stopped to watch us leave and to shout words of encouragement and pass on their best wishes. Mr. Howe hovered at the back of the crowd, noticeable by the tall hat he always wore that increased his already impressive height by another foot at least. Unwinn leant against the wall opposite; he nodded as I caught his eye, pitcher in hand.

As we walked in front, bathed in the sun's warm glow, we could hear the chattering and occasional laughter from those who followed. So pleasant it was to hear, as if death, pain and heartache were left at the perimeter wall of the last house that stood on the village edge and were for now, forgotten. So glad were we of an opportunity to celebrate, so content to experience once again the festivity that surrounds the unison of two people, rather than the sorrow that accompanies their divide. A slice of normality was offered to us this day and all who could, gladly partook of it.

Mr. Mompesson was already installed in his position when we arrived. Catherine stood at his side and raised her hand to wave energetically as we approached. The air there was unusually still, thus making the birdsong and the bubbling of the water upon the stone louder than is customary. On the grass that grew between the outcrops of limestone were dotted clusters of daffodil and crocus, the final flourishes of the season.

As we descended the embankment I noticed Mr. Daniel standing nervously at the foot of the rock face. He wore a coat with long tails, breeches and boots, his hair had been washed and brushed and on seeing Mother he stood up to attention and held her in such a tender regard, that I was at once assured as to the truth of Mother's words that night in the parlour. And so it was, that in this place of great natural beauty, my mother and Mr. Daniel exchanged vows and became man and wife.

It was a surprise to all that Mother and Mr. Daniel had indeed decided to alter slightly the traditional wording of the vows exchanged. None gathered had witnessed such a thing before. In these times however, we are becoming quite accustomed to witnessing events n'er witnessed before! Happenings prior to our affliction that might have produced outrage, contempt or at best complaint are now met with acceptance and tolerance, though they may yet not fail to raise an eyebrow.

Mother has given me the script for the ceremony, some of which was dictated by her and written in the hand of Mr. Mompesson. How secretive they have both been! Neither Catherine nor I had the slightest inclination! As a keepsake of this wonderful day I am going to attach those words. Due to our present unfortunate circumstance the service was much shorter than is usual. However, I feel this rather added to the proceedings making it, as it was, all the more personal.

Joseph managed to remain quiet during the ceremony, although he fidgeted a little to try and remove his hand from my grasp. Now, taking his first steps, he is eager to test his legs and to take advantage of his newly-found freedom. Upon completion everyone clapped and some even let out a cheer. I could not imagine such a thing occurring in church but here, today, no one seemed to mind, least of all the good reverend, who simply smiled broadly.

Once the marriage ceremony was completed, we all made our way back to the rectory and amassed in the large back garden. How fine it appeared. The table had been laid out with refreshments. What a banquet we enjoyed. Upon the table, laid on platters, were the finest cuts of cured bacon, pies both sweet and savoury, roasted meats, pickled herrings, cheese and preserved fruits. Amongst the vases of blooms and blossoms there were dotted jugs of mead, cider and ale and the bottles of wine from Chatsworth House, chosen and donated by the Earl himself. In the far corner of the garden a hog roasted upon a spit above a wood-fed fire, lit in what resembled an old tin bath. We ate, drank and chatted happily. The bride and groom were congratulated by all in turn and everyone seemed to be in good spirit. After we had chance to sate our stomachs with the delicious foods, Mr. Stanley called all to attention and made a fine speech, blessing the newlyweds to whom we all raised a glass. Thenceforth the drinking began in earnest.

In the absence of a band, Catherine directed Mr. Mompesson and the Reverend Stanley as to the relocating of the rectory clavichord. It sat thus under the sitting room window, which stood wide open, and as Catherine played as best she could, we all danced and sang. As the evening drew on, nigh all, fuelled by alcohol and infected by the exuberant atmosphere, were instilled with a newfound joy for life, we danced and sang as never before. The rules of partition were for that night forgotten, as friends and neighbours once again huddled in closed circles, arm in arm or hands upon shoulders, and thus celebrated life and love together.

As we turned and spun I threw my head back and lost my soul to the the star-ridden sky. How I wished that my own dear Rowland were by my side. I prayed silently to the heavens that fate would find it in itself to provide another night such as this, with warm air and clear skies with which to bless our own union.

At just after midnight, Mother and Mr. Daniel took their leave and retired to the house. Joseph had settled and fallen asleep in the nursery. It had been arranged that I too was to stay the night at the rectory in the guest room. Feeling exhaustion, no doubt from the preparations and the excitement of the occasion itself, I retired not long after Mother's departure. During a pause in the music I bid goodnight to Catherine and once again thanked her for all her kind efforts, to which she replied:

"My dear Emmott it is my pleasure entirely. Never did I think that I would witness such joy in the village again, how it pleases the soul and warms the heart to see it so." I smiled broadly and agreed, adding,

"Indeed, it seems that even the air is filled with joy, how sweet it smells this night."

The look that Catherine gave me upon hearing my words confused me somewhat, for her face, once light with the infectious carelessness suddenly darkened and her brow knitted in an expression of both shock and concern. Feeling, as I did, suddenly overcome with fatigue, I enquired not as to her meaning but rather retired directly to my bed.

The merrymaking continued until dawn. Unwinn passed out and slept the night slumped against the trunk of the cherry tree. As I lay in bed I could hear the laughter and boisterous exchanges from below. The villagers celebrated as never before, as if they might never have occasion to again. The ever-present threat of death under which we had all lived these past months seemed to make life that night all the sweeter. As the sun rose, the last of the revellers departed and the sounds of merriment, which had gradually become more subdued, eventually ceased altogether. As night turned into day, a short-lived silence prevailed before the birds took to the wing and filled the air with the first songs of the new day.

Mr. John Daniel & Mrs. Elizabeth Sydall.
Order Of Matrimonial Service.

Dearly beloved friends, those in body and those in spirit, we are gathered together here in the sight of God and in the face of his congregation, to join together this man and this woman in holy matrimony, which is an honourable state, instituted of God in paradise, in times of man's innocence, signifying unto us the mystical union that is betwixt Christ and his church. And therefore this holy union is not to be taken lightly or wantonly but reverently, discretely, soberly and above all else, joyfully. May these persons before me be unified in matrimony for the mutual society, help and comfort, that the one ought to have of the other, both in prosperity and adversity, into this holy state may these two persons present, come now to be joined. Therefore if any man can show any just cause, why they may not lawfully be joined together let him now speak, or else ever after hold his peace.

Wilt thou, Elizabeth Sydall, have this man, John Daniel, to thy wedded husband, to live together after God's ordinance in the holy state of matrimony? Wilt thou obey him and serve him, love, honour and keep him, in sickness and in health. And forsaking all others, keep thee only to him so long as ye both shall live?

Wilt thou, John Daniel, have this woman, Elizabeth Sydall, to thy wedded wife, to live together after God's ordinance in the holy state of matrimony? Wilt thou love her, comfort her, honour and keep her, in sickness and in health. And forsaking all others, keep thee only to her so long as ye both shall live?

I, John Daniel, take thee, Elizabeth Sydall, to my wedded wife, to have and to hold, from this day forward, for better, for worse, for richer, for poorer, in sickness and in health, to love and to cherish 'til death us depart, according to God's holy ordinance and thereto I give thee my troth.

I, Elizabeth Sydall, do take thee, John Daniel, to my lawful wedded husband, to have and to hold from this day forward, for better, for worse, for richer, for poorer, in sickness and in health, to love, to cherish and to obey 'til death us depart. With God's will may we build a life together from these dark beginnings that is full of hope, wonder and joy. May our past sorrows permit us hence to be ever more thankful for what we have this day been given and may we never be ignorant to the preciousness of the present moment. May those beloved and lost to us look down with compassion upon us this day and bless our happy union. May all this be done according to

God's holy ordinance and thereto I give thee my troth.

Wilt thou have this woman to thy wife?

Wilt thou have this man to thy husband?

With this ring I thee wed: with my body I thee worship and with all my worldly goods I thee endow. In the name of the Father and the Son and the Holy Ghost. Amen.

O eternal God, creator and preserver of all mankind, giver of all spiritual grace. The author of everlasting life: send thy blessing upon these thy servants, this man and this woman, whom we bless in thy name, that as Isaac and Rebecca lived faithfully together, so these persons may surely perform and keep the vow and covenant betwixt them made, whereof this ring given and received, is a token and pledge, and may ever remain in perfect love and peace together, and live according unto thy laws, through Jesus Christ our lord. Amen.

Those whom God hath joined together, let no man put a sunder.

For as much as John Daniel and Elizabeth Sydall have consented together in holy wedlock, and have witnessed the same before God, and this company, and thereto have given and pledged their both either to other and have declared the same by giving and receiving of a ring, and by joining of hands, I pronounce that they be man and wife together. In the name of the Father, of the Son and of the Holy Ghost. Amen.

May God bless us all here gathered, may he fill our lives with fortitude and resilience in these times of great sorrows. May he plant the seed of hope in our heart that it might grow there and flourish and bare forth the promise of happier days to come. Today we all bare testimony to this happy union, let us put for a short time our woes aside and rejoice, one and all, in the matrimony of our dear brethren: John and Elizabeth.

John and Elizabeth, in union from this day forth, I bestow upon you my most sincere blessing. May your days together surpass your greatest expectations. May peace and love be with you always. Man and wife.

27th April 1666

I have felt rather out of sorts today and although I managed this morning to aid Catherine in the cleaning and tidying of the remnants of yesterday's festivities, it was with a heavy head and a tiredness of limbs. When finally the debris had been cleared, seeing my disposition, Catherine insisted that I return home to rest, declaring that the events of the last few days had surely taken their toll upon me. I took Joseph up into my arms with some effort, so weak did I feel. As we left I perceived that same look of anxiety marked upon her features as I had experienced the previous night. As to reassure her, I bid her farewell as brightly as I was able and walked purposefully down the pathway that led to the front gate, observed all the while by Catherine standing still at the threshold. Once having turned the corner, out of sight, I sat a while on the stone wall, Joseph upon my lap. So installed, I waited to catch my breath and for the dizziness and nausea

I felt to abate. Once sufficiently recovered, I returned home directly and have since taken to my bed.

Mother has come to call on me frequently and I see the same look of anguish upon her face as I witnessed in Catherine's this morning. I am fretful about missing my tryst with Rowland but cannot ask Mother to go in my place or even confide in her my concern, she being ignorant of our arrangement. I have begun to feel feverish and my head aches so that I find it difficult to maintain my train of thought. My arm is so heavy that the mere act of writing I find to be most laborious. I hope that after a good night's rest I will awake to find myself quite recovered and that it is, as Catherine asserted, only the events of the last few days that have depleted me thus. I have one desire now and that is to sleep.

April 1666

I awoke to find Mother at my bedside. I had no idea as to the time of day or night it might be, or indeed whether it be morning or afternoon. I am taken with a fever that rages through each and every part of my body, burning so hot that the sweat pours from me in rivulets. Then, in turn, I feel an icy coldness in my veins, so entrenched that no matter how I try I cannot warm myself but take to shivering beneath my covers. I have periods of wakefulness and clarity but am helpless to fight off the heavy drowsiness that pulls me once again back into sleep.

Catherine visited this evening. I am unsure as to how long she rested at my bedside but on awaking one time I noticed the sky to be a pitch black outside of my window. I summoned the strength to pull this journal from under my mattress and instructed her that, should I not be able to do so myself, it must find its way to Rowland. She, of course, recognised it at once and upon opening the front cover she read her own inscription. How unaware at the time of writing those words was she of the horrors that would be recorded within these pages. I saw a tear run from her cheek, as it fell it blotted the ink that lay upon the open page. As she closed the pages I plied it gently from her hand and returned it to its hiding place. As I did so, I noticed a large, purple blemish upon my arm. How similar it was, I thought, to the tear blotted ink. Strangely it did not alarm me, so weak and nauseous did I feel. I lay my head back upon my pillow and drifted back into sleep, Catherine holding my hand all the while.

The next time I awoke it was Mother who was again at my side. She wiped my brow with a wet piece of cloth, so tender were her actions that they at once soothed me. I could hear, but not understand, her gentle words as she rolled me over so she might change the stinking, sweat-drenched sheets upon which I lay.

It is dark now and I find myself alone. I am unsure as to whether it be the same night or a different one.

April 1666

The fever is upon me. To write is both a physical and mental struggle. Mother is here and then she is gone. I am trying to tell her that all is well but she looks at me with apprehension and misunderstanding. She tells me that my words are senseless but to me they speak truth. I have glimpsed death often in my sleep state, though it is not a sleep like I have ever known before. My soul, it seems to journey to a place that is no place, for it has no physical reality. It is deep blue calm. Warmth. Comfort. Love. Home.

April 1666

I fear this will be my final entry. I cannot describe the effort it takes for me to write this now, I summon strength from somewhere. My waking body is consumed with an overriding exhaustion. More often than not I am no longer here but in some dream-like state in which my being is so massive that there is no room for anything external to it. In this state there is immeasurable peace and rest, but unwillingly, still, from time to time, I am pulled crudely back into this harsh, cold and pain-ridden reality which is my body, so weak that the softest of footsteps vibrates through its every nerve and fibre and each word uttered is a long-lost tongue, struggled over until at last it is made sense of. Sometimes I am confused, I know not what is real and what is in my mind, the two seem to be growing ever more intertwined. So burdensome is the reality of the physical now that I am impatient to once again become that swollen entity which is pulled ever stronger and faster, as a cloud gathering speed upon a strengthening wind, to the sweetest of surrenders. It becomes more and more difficult to resist this journey's end. I feel

God all around me; or rather when my soul rises from the sheath of skin that is my body, we dissolve together into a wonderful union of homecoming, the solace of which is beyond any description, beyond any words.

I want you to know, Rowland, that at present I am lucid in my thoughts. You are the first thought on waking to reality, ever near me, ever with me, and you are my last before I drift thankfully, back into oblivion. Be not sad my love when I tell you that in that other reality there is no thought for you or for anyone else, those that matter most here are there discarded, rather as a child's outgrown toy. This, it seems, is the nature of dying, so we leave peaceably and without regret. Unfortunately my love, those left behind are not bequeathed the same gift. Take solace my love, in the fact that I am almost gone, I go not in fear but in calm acceptance. Lying in this bed I have tried to relive every moment of our time together, from our very first meeting to the last time I set my eyes upon you and with heavy heart, turned from you for the very last time, knowing, as I believe I did then, that we would not meet again in this life.

I have entrusted my very dear friend Catherine with the safe keeping of this journal. She has assured me that upon my passing she will do all in her power to ensure it finds itself delivered into your hands; it is the only place I would have it be.

I grow weaker by the minute so, my love, I will bid you farewell and give you my heartfelt thanks for your love, your kindness and for making me so very happy.

My dearest Rowland, I beg of you, be not afraid of death, yet more importantly my love, be not afraid of life.

Yours always,

Emmott.

LINDA COPP

Epilogue.

Emmott Sydall died on the 29th April 1666.

Between 7th September 1665 and 1st of November of the following year a total of two hundred and sixty men, women and children fell victim to the plague. It is believed that the courage and actions of the people of this small Derbyshire village prevented the spread of this horrific disease to neighbouring towns and villages. Who can say how many lives were spared by their selfless actions?

Unfortunately, Catherine Mompesson did not live to see the end of that awful time in Eyam's history; her conviction on bidding her children farewell, that they would not be reunited in this world, proved to be correct. Catherine Mompesson died on the 25th August 1666. Although not from Eyam herself, her husband felt it only right that her final resting place should be found in the graveyard of Eyam church. After the plague, William Mompesson commissioned a fitting memorial to his beloved wife; every year on 'Plague Sunday' a bouquet of red roses is placed upon her tomb.

The Reverend Mompesson and their two children survived. William Mompesson continued his ministry in the parish of Eyam for a further three years, helping to rebuild the community that had been so desolated. In 1669, he moved to Eakring in Nottinghamshire and shortly after was remarried. He and his new wife, Elizabeth, went on to have four children, two girls and two boys. Unfortunately both of the boys died in infancy.

John Daniel perished in July 1666. Emmott's mother, Elizabeth Daniel, was one of the plague's final casualties and passed on 17th October 1666. She was survived by her infant child, Joseph, who was cared for, as had been formerly arranged on her deathbed and testified by the Reverend Stanley, by her friend and neighbour Rebecca Hawkesworth, to whom she left her estate in return for the undertaking.

Marshall Howe remained a resident of Eyam for many years after the plague. He was remarried six years later to a Mary Hadfield, thought to be a relative of Alexander Hadfield, owner of the house into which the plague first entered and so claimed its first victim, their lodger Mr. Viccars. Alexander Hadfield also succumbed on 3rd August 1666.

Marshall Howe died in 1698. However, for some generations after the plague his somewhat gruesome reputation lived on; parents would use his name and threaten to call upon him to tame their unruly children.

Matthew Morten of Shepherd's Flatt was the only survivor amongst his family, losing his wife Margaret and three children. He lived alone for some time with his greyhound, Flash, and his small herd of cows for company. Shortly after the plague had ceased to claim any further victims, it is told that one afternoon, whilst Matthew was sitting outside of his home, Flash excitedly ran up to a lonely female figure walking up the road, supposedly mistaking her for his dead mistress. The woman in question was Sarah Hawkesworth whose husband Peter was the third victim of the plague. From this chance encounter a friendship grew and the two were later married.

The Reverend Stanley stayed on in Eyam until his death on St. Bartholomew's Day 1670. Although not buried in the churchyard in Eyam, there is a memorial stone dedicated to him to be found there.

Rowland Torre came to Eyam and to the Sydall house on the very day the Cordon Sanitaire was lifted, only to find it empty and abandoned. He no doubt had his fears confirmed as to the fate of Emmott and her family by a surviving resident of the village. There is no record as to what became of Emmott's sweetheart Rowland Torre and if indeed he ever married.

LINDA COPP

Afterword.

My inspiration for the writing of this book was derived from a chance visit to Eyam whilst touring the Peak District in a camper van. The tragic tale of this small and enchanting village moved me deeply. If you happen across it, just off the A623, the village has a museum which tells the story of the plague years. In the quiet, narrow streets, the 'Plague Cottages' are marked with plaques commemorating the families that perished therein. From the village square you can climb the half mile to the 'Riley Graves' close to Riley House Farm. Here are buried seven members of the Hancock family. Elizabeth Hancock had the traumatic and gruesome task of digging the graves singlehandedly and subsequently laying to rest her husband and six children, who all died within a week of one another. Many families were at best fractured by the plague but the 'Riley Graves' are a solemn indictment to the complete decimation experienced by the less fortunate of households.

In another direction you can take the walk to Cucklett Delf (the crag of limestone indeed bares an eerie resemblance to a skull) where, during the self-imposed 'Cordon Sanitaire', the open services were held and from there on to the boundary stone, the secret meeting place where Emmott Sydall would stand and wave to her sweetheart, Rowland Torre.

Acknowledgements and Further Reading.

Eyam Plague 1665-1666 by John Clifford.

The History and Antiquities Of Eyam: With a Full and Particular Account of the Great Plague, Which Desolated That Village 1666 by William Wood.

Eyam The Plague by Clarence Daniel.

Eyam Plague Village by David Paul.

A Journal of the Plague Year by Daniel Defoe.

Acknowledgements

The publisher would like to thank Russell Spencer, Matt Vidler, Laura-Jayne Humphrey, Lianne Bailey-Woodward, Leonard West, Katie Major, Janelle Hope and Susan Woodard for their hard work and efforts in bringing this book to publication.

LINDA COPP

About the Publisher

LR Price Publications is dedicated to publishing books by unknown authors.

We use a mixture of traditional and modern publishing methods to bring our authors' words to the wider world.

We print, publish, distribute and market books in a variety of formats including paper and hard back, electronic books e-books, digital audio books and online.

If you are an author interested in getting your book published; or a book retailer interested in selling our books, please contact us.

www.lrpricepublications.com

L.R. Price Publications Ltd,

27 Old Gloucester Street,

London, WC1N 3AX.

(0203) 051 9572 publishing@lrprice.com

Milton Keynes UK
Ingram Content Group UK Ltd.
UKHW021051131123
432477UK00016B/1119